Second Chance Valentine

Second Chance Valentine

Ocean City Boardwalk Series
Book 7

Donna Fasano

Find the author:

Facebook – Facebook.com/DonnaFasanoAuthor

Twitter – Twitter.com/DonnaFaz

Pinterest – Pinterest.com/DonnaFaz

Instagram – Instagram.com/Donna_Fasano

Newsletter Sign-up – http://madmimi.com/signups/110899/
join

Contents

Chapter One

Even though Atlantic General Hospital was at least seven miles from the ocean, Josie could still smell a salty tang lacing the frigid winter air as she stepped out of her car and hurried toward the entrance of the ER. The briny scent drew on deeply embedded adolescent memories like a thick tap root, some conjuring a homey, cozy feeling, others bleak and depressing and filled with heartache. She shook off the distraction with a tiny jerk of her head. She needed to get to Grams.

The automatic glass doors slid open and Josie squinted against the bright fluorescent lights blaring from overhead. A young woman sat behind the desk, staring at a computer screen as she rapidly tapped on the keyboard.

"Excuse me," Josie said. "I'm here to see Deloris Baxter."

"Are you a family member?" The woman didn't look up from her computer screen.

"Yes," Josie assured her. "I'm her granddaughter."

"Go over to the waiting room," she instructed. "I'll have someone come to escort you back to see her."

Anxiety planted Josie to the spot. "Can you tell me anything? Is Grams okay?"

The woman sighed, her gaze dragging up to meet Josie's. "Hon, I have to get this information into the system so a patient can be treated. But I give you my word that I'll have someone come to talk to you. It'll be just a minute or two."

Josie nodded and then turned on her heel. *A minute or two*, she silently chanted the words, mentally clutching the promise. She could quell this worry for two more minutes. The waiting room was just down the corridor. She stood in the doorway, frowning, concern turning her brain into a quagmire that made the simplest of decisions impossible, like which chair to sit in.

"Josie?"

Her attention swung to the right.

Meeting Alex Thompson's sea green eyes had her lips parting, but no sound came out. His deep brown hair had been raked straight back from his forehead and a shadow of whiskers darkened his jaw. The last time she'd seen him, his boyish good looks had attracted more than his fair share of female attention. The passing years had tamed his more coltish features by honing the planes and hollows of his face. The result made him even more handsome.

"Alex." She blinked. "What are you doing here?"

"Waiting for you, I guess. I called 911 for Deloris. I followed the ambulance over."

Confusion tangled Josie's thoughts like a snarled ball of yarn. Alex had been at the diner? But he owned a restaurant of his own. A swanky place in West Ocean City.

"You were eating at Joe's Place?"

"Working," he corrected her. "I was working there."

Josie's gaze darted to the wadded white apron sitting on top of his coat on the side table.

He eased his six foot frame from the chair. "Deloris and I had just finished dinner service. We were cleaning up a bit and discussing tomorrow's menu when she complained of jaw pain. She looked pale and totally exhausted."

Alex Thompson was working in Grams's kitchen? The absurdity of the notion had her frown deepening.

"Where's your mom, Josie? Deloris told me to call your mom."

Fist-size gold nuggets washing up on the shore wouldn't have been enough to get Josie's mother to return to Ocean City.

"Mom's not coming," she told him. "I'm here, though."

His mouth went flat. "Does she know this is Deloris's second visit to the ER in the past few months?"

The news made Josie suck in a startled breath.

"She must realize her mother is in her seventies," he barreled ahead. "Does she know Deloris is at that diner all hours of the day and night? That she's working herself to death? Something's got to be done."

"I-I didn't know," she stammered. "Alex, I talk to Grams at least twice a month. She never said a word."

"Of course, she didn't. The woman is stubborn as a mule."

The description fit Grams to a T. It fit her mother, too. Josie had always put it down to apples and trees and all that.

"Pain in her jaw," Josie murmured. "Sounds like a heart attack."

Alex sighed. "It does. But they wouldn't tell me anything. A doctor came out once, and twice a nurse came, looking for a family member. Deloris has been back there for five hours, Josie."

"I got here as fast as I could," she told him. "I was just getting off work in Rockville when Mom called me. I drove home. Dropped my cat off at my neighbor's with a bag of food. Threw some clothes into an overnight case. The traffic around DC was horrendous. Route 50 was clear, though. It's a wonder I didn't get pulled over. I was driving crazy fast. The girl at the desk told me someone would be coming out. Soon. In a minute or two."

The instant she realized she was babbling, she clamped her mouth shut.

Silence had barely settled around them when he said, "Last fall, Deloris had a minor heart attack."

Josie stopped chewing her lip long enough to mutter, "Why didn't she tell me?"

"She was in the hospital for a couple of days. I tried my darnedest to make her take some time off to recuperate, but she was back in the diner a few days later. I don't think she was ready."

The sigh issuing from Josie was tight with guilt. "I wish she'd have told me."

"She's the most hardheaded woman I have ever met."

Josie only nodded in response. "How bad was she? When you called the ambulance, I mean? Was she conscious?"

"Oh, she was not only conscious, she was cussing a blue streak. Thank goodness the last customer had already left."

The tension in his face eased and Josie watched a grin quirk one corner of his mouth. Her gaze lingered on his lips a moment longer than it should have. As if there were suddenly too little oxygen in the air, she experienced an odd wooziness.

"She *really* didn't want me calling for help." He actually chuckled. "She kept insisting she was fine. I thought she was going to smack me. She was furious. I'm sure she'll fire me before this is over with, but that's all right. She's where she needs to be." He heaved a sigh and combed his fingers through his dark hair. "She can't fire me tonight. That's all that matters for now. I'll worry about tomorrow later."

Josie inhaled deeply and widened her eyes, scrambling to recover her equilibrium. Alex glanced toward the front desk and then at his watch, seemingly unaware of her unsteadiness. Thank heavens.

Then his eyes met hers and he was quiet for the length of two heartbeats. He tilted his head to one side.

"Are you okay?"

He reached for her, his palms sliding over her shoulders.

"I'm fine," she said. "Really. Just worried. And tired."

"You had a long drive. And of course, you're worried. You look like you need to sit." He guided her to the chair he'd vacated.

She was close enough to feel the warmth of him, to smell the slightly smoky scent that clung to his clothing from cooking in the diner. A comfortable, homey aroma.

He squatted in front of her, reaching across her to the table where his jacket and apron lay.

"Here," he said, tucking a small, plastic bottle into her hand. "An orderly came by earlier, passing these out. I haven't opened it. Take a drink of water. It'll make you feel better."

Just to have something to do, Josie twisted off the cap and lifted the bottle to her lips. The water was room temperature, but it tasted good. She realized she hadn't had anything to drink or eat since lunch time.

"Thank you." She lifted her chin and looked into his face only to find him studying her intently.

His shoulders sagged a fraction and the tension in his face eased. The smallest of smiles played across his mouth.

"You look good, Josie."

He'd spoken so softly she wasn't certain she'd heard him correctly.

"You're just as beautiful as ever."

The words startled her. They startled him as well, that much was clear. The whispery smile disappeared and his spine straightened. Their gazes held one more awkward second before he directed his eyes at his watch and stood up. Unwittingly, Josie's focused attention followed him.

Had he really just called her beautiful?

"I was hoping to stay long enough to get an update," he said, his voice clear and distinct. "But I really should get home. Emma's been with a neighbor."

"Oh, your daughter." Josie stood up so quickly water sloshed from the mouth of the bottle onto the back of her hand. "Of course, you should go home."

"I'm sure she was fed dinner. We texted back and forth a bit ago."

He reached for his coat and apron, and again, they were close enough that she could feel the heat of his body.

"But it's way past her bed time," he added.

"I understand."

"If something happens and you need me during the night," Alex said, "don't hesitate to call."

"Thanks. I appreciate that."

They quickly exchanged cell numbers.

"Tell Deloris not to worry about Joe's Place," Alex said. "I'll open as usual tomorrow morning. Sunday hours are short. Just breakfast and lunch. I can handle things by myself, I think." He shrugged into his coat. "Then we'll be closed until Thursday. We'll have a few days to reassess the situation."

"Winter schedule," Josie murmured. From somewhere in the recesses of her mind, she remembered Grams opened the diner from Thursday to Sunday during the winter season when the town was devoid of tourists.

"Right." He nodded. "You'll be okay here?"

Josie arched her brows. "It won't be the first time I've faced the dragon alone."

He chuckled, but his quick glance toward the door leading outside told her he was eager to get home to his daughter.

"I'll be fine," she assured him. "Thank you, Alex. For being with Grams. For calling for help. And for staying until I could get here. I really appreciate all you've done."

With a final nod, he stuffed the balled up apron under his arm and turned away from her.

Her gaze riveted to the broad expanse of his back as she absently screwed the lid back onto the bottle of water she held. If someone had told her she'd come face to face with Alex Thompson tonight, she'd have never believed it. Just as incredible had been learning that he worked as a cook at the diner. The situation still seemed inconceivable to her.

He looked good. Better than good, really. Josie licked at her dry lips.

"You're just as beautiful as ever."

His compliment rolled over her like a thick sea mist. It should have made her smile. She should have felt flattered, but a murky emotion she couldn't quite name churned in her chest instead.

Second Chance Valentine

When Alex reached the exit, he turned, and she felt heat rush to her face at being caught staring. He lifted his hand and she raised hers in return. He trudged out into the cold night. Then she watched the doors slide shut behind the reason she'd spent the past dozen or so years steering clear of Ocean City, Maryland.

Chapter Two

Josie stood at the doorway of the small exam room. With her eyes closed, Grams would have looked in peaceful slumber had it not been for the medical equipment creating an arc around the head of the gurney. Monitors beeped and clicked, and two bags of clear fluid released steady drips that ran through the tubes connected to Grams, one on the crook of her arm, the other on the back of her hand. Blue veins trailed beneath papery white skin. Helpless and vulnerable were not words Josie would have ever used to describe Grams. Until tonight.

Tears welled and burned Josie's eye sockets, but she blinked them away, determined to remain strong for Grams.

It wasn't until she moved closer to the gurney that she saw the nurse making notes on a medical chart.

"Excuse me," Josie whispered. "Can you tell me how she's doing?"

The nurse looked up and smiled. "You are—" She thumbed through the papers clipped to the folder. "Here it is. You're Peg Baxter?"

"No. Peg is my mother." Josie gently touched the metal footboard of the gurney. "I'm Deloris Baxter's granddaughter."

Regret pulled at the nurse's mouth. "I'm sorry. The privacy laws are strict these days. Do you want me to wake Mrs. Baxter to ask—"

"No, no." Josie shook her head vehemently. "Let her rest."

The woman flipped the chart closed and tucked the pen into her pocket. "Well, we'll have to wake her soon, anyway. Now that someone is here, the doctor is going to want to come back in. He left in a bit of a huff." She offered Josie a tight-lipped smile.

"Grams was being uncooperative?" It was an easy guess for Josie.

"Oh, you could say that." The nurse's pretty blue eyes widened as she spoke. She closed the space between herself and Josie. "Listen, can we ask you for a favor? When the doctor comes back in here, will you help him talk your grandmother into allowing us to admit her? She needs observation. And we'd like her to see the cardiologist tomorrow." The nurse glanced toward the bed. "She's determined to check herself out of here. And that's the last thing she needs right now."

Josie nodded and promised, "I'll do everything I can to help."

"Thanks. I'm going to go see if I can find Dr. Elkins." The nurse skirted around Josie and hurried out the door.

Josie had barely had time to round the bed before her grandmother's eyes fluttered open.

"Grams? Hey. How are you feeling?"

"Is she gone?"

The question startled Josie and she wondered if her grandmother might be a little disoriented.

"Gone? Who?" she asked.

"The nurse," Grams said. "The woman wouldn't stop yammering at me. 'You need to stay here for a few days. You have to see the cardiologist. You need to change your diet. You're going to have to retire soon. You can't work so hard.' Yada-yada-yada."

Josie's jaw dropped open a little. "Grams! You were faking sleep?"

"Of course, I was," Grams grumbled. "No one could actually fall asleep on this blasted sheet of stainless steel they've chained me to."

"You ought to be ashamed."

"Oh, sweetie pie, my shame glands shriveled up years ago." Her gaze darted from one side rail to the other. "I want to sit up. I hate being flat on my back. Makes me feel at a disadvantage."

Josie found the electronic controller in the rumpled sheet and hit the button that caused the head of the bed to lift.

"So your mother couldn't be bothered to come, I see," Grams muttered.

"When she called me, we decided it was best for me to come."

There was no humor in her grandmother's sharp bark of laughter.

"I'll bet that's what '*we*' decided." She fidgeted, tugging at the sheet. "How about Alex? Is he still here? The two of you need to get me out of this place."

"Alex went home."

Grams harrumphed. "Why am I not surprised? It's *his* fault I'm in this predicament. He probably heard I'm determined to go home and he slunk away like a—"

"He did not slink away, Grams," Josie said. "And your being here is not his fault. You needed medical attention and he saw that you got it. In my opinion, that makes him a hero." Deeming that her grandmother wasn't showing appreciation for her situation, Josie added, "He stayed in that waiting room for five hours. He wanted to stay for an update, but he had to get home to Emma. You know, his *daughter?*"

"All right. All right," Grams said. "So he had to go home. But that doesn't change the fact that I need to get out of here." She looked up at Josie. "You heard that nurse. They want me to spend the night."

The final three words were spoken as though the mere idea was cruel and unusual punishment. Josie's spine straightened of its own volition.

"I heard every word the nurse said." She tipped up her chin. "And I think you should listen to the professionals. Let them watch you tonight. See the specialist in the morning."

"I will do no such thing." Indignation inserted more oomph into the words. "Except for the few nights your granddaddy and I were on our honeymoon, I have slept every night in our bed. Tonight will be no different, missy." Grams stretched her arm out straight. "Get this tape off here. And find my clothes. I have a diner to open first thing in the morning."

Josie fell silent and went motionless. Her grandmother was going to do it. She intended to pull out those needles and walk out of the emergency room. And there wasn't a darn thing Josie could say or do to stop her.

A fearful emotion, strong and abrupt, swept through her whole body. Tears rushed to her eyes, blurring her vision, and she trembled.

"Grams, please." Josie choked out the words. "I need you to stay. I need to know you're all right. I need to know you're being taken care of."

Her grandmother looked into her face, her arm lowering to her side.

"Alex told me to tell you he'll open the diner in the morning," she rushed to continue. "And I'll help him, Grams. I promise. I'll stay in Ocean City for a while. I've got some vacation time due me. I can stay a week. Or two. Heck, I can stay the whole month of February, if need be." She let the tears roll down her face, unheeded. "Please let me help you. I need to know you're okay, Grams."

"Oh, now... I'll be fine, Josie."

"We don't know that for certain." She swallowed around the painful lump in her throat. "I feel so guilty. I need more time."

"Time?" Her voice was feather soft. "I don't understand. What do you mean?"

"You can't..." The word that rose up in her throat stuck there like a barbed fish hook. "I don't want you to... go anywhere."

"Stop, now," Grams said. "I'm not going anywhere."

"I should have done more than just call you on the phone. Alex was right. I should have been coming to visit you. I should have come around." She sniffled, unable to quell the tremor of her bottom lip. The metal of the side rail was cool when she rested her hand on it. "I don't know what I would do if something happened to you."

The determination in her grandmother's expression softened and she slid her warm, dry fingers over Josie's.

"Don't cry, sweetheart," Grams said. "You've been busy living your life. Just like I've been busy living mine. It's no reason to feel guilty. I'm going to be fine. A little heart misbehavior can't get the best of me. You know that. I'm healthy as a horse."

But the assurances weren't enough to alleviate Josie's worry, or her tears. In silent response, she just offered a slow, small shake of her head to express her disbelief as her tears continued to roll.

Finally, Grams relented. "Okay, Jojo. I'll stay."

Chapter Three

The next morning, Josie locked the door of her grandmother's apartment located above the diner. She'd come in and out of this door hundreds, no, thousands of times during her summertime stays with Grams as a child and through her early teen years.

She could tell Alex had already arrived and was busy in the kitchen downstairs because the rich scent of freshly brewed coffee wafted in the frosty air. She pulled the facings of her coat closed and headed down the stairs, her breath billowing in lacy mist.

It had taken hours last night for Grams to be admitted to the hospital, and Josie had stayed until she'd gotten settled in her room. The doctor had been surprised by the change in his patient's attitude about remaining overnight for observation and he'd spent some time checking her over before promising Grams that he would set up an appointment with the cardiologist.

Josie's tears had affected her grandmother. Profoundly. On only rare occasions as a kid had Grams called her *Jojo*. Josie had been six or seven the summer that Misty, a beautiful grey cat that hung around the diner, had been struck by a car in the parking lot. Grams had pulled Josie onto her lap and crooned, "*I'm sorry, Jojo,*" over and over, as she'd rocked her distraught granddaughter. And at the end of every summer when Josie was about to leave, Grams never failed to kiss her cheek and say, "*You be good now, Jojo.*" Nine times out of ten, Josie had been crying as she'd reluctantly crawled into the back seat of the car that would take her home to her mother. Oh, how she'd hated to leave Grams.

She rounded the front corner of the building and passed the large window and Josie smiled as she saw "Joe's Place" painted in neat, red letters across the plate glass. The diner had been Joseph Baxter's pride and joy. Josie's memory of the man was fuzzy. The descriptions that came to mind were big, gentle, and jovial. The thought reminded

Josie that there had been another time when Grams had lovingly called her Jojo... at Granddaddy's funeral.

Shaking off the melancholy, Josie pulled open the front door and was hit in the face with delectable smells of bacon, onions, and rich, savory spices.

"Good morning," she called.

The booths and tables were empty, but a little girl sat on a stool at the counter, a fat backpack leaning against the wall.

"Hey, there," Josie greeted. "You must be Emma."

The child smiled at her, nodding. With her light green eyes and shiny, dark hair, she was the spitting image of her father.

Emma set down the felt-tipped pen she'd been using to doodle on a sketch pad. "And you're Miss Deloris's granddaughter."

"I am," she confirmed. When she got close, she reached out her hand. "Glad to meet you, Emma. I'm Josie." They shook hands. "You're up awfully early. It's Sunday. Shouldn't you be sleeping in?"

Emma rolled her eyes. "I wish. I never get to sleep in on Sundays. Daddy's got to be at work early." She picked up the pen. "But it's not so bad today. I'm going shopping with my friend Chloe. Her mom is picking me up later. We're going up to Rehoboth to the outlet shops."

"Ooo, the big outlets." Josie let her eyes go round.

Ocean City had a small center of nice outlet shops in the west part of town, but they couldn't compare to the three different centers full of stores located in Rehoboth Beach, Delaware about thirty miles north.

The little girl's green eyes danced. "Dad gave me some money for a new outfit."

"Girl," Josie said with just the right amount of envy in her voice, "I would much rather go shopping with you than work here today."

Emma giggled.

"Listen, I'm headed to the kitchen for a cup of coffee and a quick talk with your dad before customers start coming in." Josie rounded the counter. "You want a glass of juice?"

"Daddy's working on breakfast," Emma told her. "I usually make my own. I like to roll up my sleeves and do for myself. But Dad thought it would be best if I stayed out of the kitchen this morning." Her dark brows arched and her voice lowered. "Just in case Miss Deloris was, um, cranky when she got here."

Josie grinned. "That was a good plan. But you can relax. Miss Deloris won't be coming in today."

Florescent fixtures blared overhead, lighting up the kitchen. Alex used a long, stainless steel spatula to remove what looked like a full pound of crisp bacon strips from the flat top griddle and set them on a draining rack. Then he picked up a second spatula, this one shorter and rounder, to turn three golden pancakes cooking on the grill. With all the equipment running, the kitchen must have been twenty degrees warmer than the dining area.

"Morning," Josie said.

He turned. "Josie."

"I just met your daughter out there. She's cute as she can be."

"Thanks." He beamed.

"I get the impression she's an independent little fireball."

Alex laughed. "That she is. She's twelve, but most days I suspect she's going on twenty-nine." He ripped a piece of aluminum foil from the roll and covered a large, stainless steel bowl filled with crispy hash browns. "She's a great kid. I'm a proud papa and I don't mind who knows it." Without skipping a beat, he added another pound of bacon to the griddle. "I expected Deloris to show up this morning. How's she doing?"

"She's good." Josie went to the coffee pot. "Well, good is a relative term, right?" She told him what little the ER doc had explained, that the heart attack had been mild and that the nitroglycerin he'd prescribed would open up the blood vessels. "We'll know more once she sees the cardiologist today."

"Like I told you last night, I've got this place covered," he assured her. "Are you taking Deloris to the doctor? Wait. It's Sunday. Doctors don't have office hours on Sunday."

Josie poured coffee into a heavy ceramic mug. "I suppose the doctor who will see her today is on call at the hospital."

Alex turned his whole body to face her. "I don't understand. She agreed to go back to the hospital today? That's a surprise."

"No." She sipped at the liquid and savored the fact that it was just as she liked it, rich, strong, black, and smooth. She swallowed. "I got her to agree to be admitted to the hospital last night."

"You're kidding me. Woman, your powers of persuasion are awesome."

His effusive tone had her smiling. Noticing the smoke rising from the griddle, she arched her brows and pointed. "Um, the pancakes?"

"The pancakes!" He scooped up the scorched circles and flipped them into the trash. "I can't believe I burned Emma's breakfast. I guess I'm more rattled than I imagined."

"Relax," she told him. "I'm your backup today."

"You don't say?" He ladled more batter onto the hot griddle.

Josie nodded. "That was the only way she'd stay. I promised to be your right-hand man."

His eyes went soft and he smiled. "In that case, welcome to Joe's Place."

The heat that rushed through her entire body caused perspiration to break out on her brow and the back of her neck. She'd have liked to blame the flush of heat on the sizzling griddle, the hot ovens, and the blazing Salamander, but she knew there was only one reason and one reason alone—Alex's smile.

* * *

It was nearly two in the afternoon when the last customer left the diner.

"We're empty," Josie called out to Alex. "I'm locking the front door before anyone else comes in." She flipped the dead bolt and turned over the sign that read CLOSED. Then she went back to wiping down the table she'd just cleared of dirty dishes, juice glasses, coffee cups, and cutlery.

Alex was drying his hands on a white cotton tea towel when he entered the dining room.

"I think I did okay, don't you?" she asked. She slid the salt and pepper shakers to the center of the table. "We were pretty busy, and I only got one order wrong. The guy wasn't too upset."

"You did great." Alex tucked one corner of the towel under the string of his apron. "I don't want to burst your bubble, but Sundays are slow. This one was no exception."

"Really?"

He nodded. "You'll see. Thursday, Friday, and Saturday we'll serve a lot more customers."

The thought made Josie groan. "My feet are killing me. How will I survive?"

Alex chuckled as he pulled out a chair from a nearby table. "Come here," he told her. "Sit for a few minutes."

She didn't wait for a second invitation. She tossed her cleaning cloth on the table and slid into the chair. His hand came down to rest on her shoulder and Josie reached up to toy with the menagerie of thin bracelets he wore on his wrist.

"Tell me about these," she said.

Alex chuckled as he pulled his hand up to show off the handmade jewelry. "Deloris bought Emma a jewelry making kit for Christmas. These two are friendship bracelets. And this one—" he gave a little tug on the elastic band "—was Emma's first attempt at stringing those little glass beads. She was proud of it." He let his hand drop to his side. "I'll ask her to make you one, if you like. I'm sure she'll jump at the chance."

"I'd like that." She inhaled deeply and let the breath rush from her, her shoulders rolling forward. "If my feet could utter a sigh of relief, they would."

Josie had been running from the dining room to the kitchen and back again since this morning. There had been a short lull around eleven when she'd shared lunch with Alex, a moist and tender chicken breast slathered with a spicy mesquite barbeque sauce served on a toasted Kaiser roll. The break had lasted all of ten minutes before customers looking for lunch started coming in.

"Alex, I can't imagine Grams on her feet all

hours of the day," Josie said. "Why doesn't she hire wait staff?"

He sat in the chair across from her. "It's off-season. In order to turn a profit in the dead of winter, you have to work with a skeleton crew."

"You and Grams? That's two bones, not a skeleton."

Alex laughed, and the rich, warm sound of it made Josie smile.

"We survive," he told her. "We share something, Deloris and I. We have a passion for feeding people."

After a moment, Josie asked him the question that had been burning in her brain since last night. "What's the story behind you're working for Grams? The last I'd heard, you owned a really nice restaurant in West Ocean City."

His green eyes darkened and he glanced off toward the far corner of the room.

"I'm sorry, Alex," she rushed to say. "If you'd rather not discuss it..."

"No. It's all right. I don't mind talking about it."

Josie rested her hands in her lap, waiting.

"A little over four years ago," he began, "my wife, Carin, was diagnosed with a brain tumor. A glioblastoma. We had terrible health insurance; I had to fight for every surgery, every treatment option, every medication. Between Carin and Emma and the restaurant, I thought I was going to go absolutely insane."

"I can't even imagine," Josie breathed.

"Carin died about two and a half years ago."

Pain etched his features and Josie's heart broke for him.

"It was hard," he said. "The hardest thing I've ever gone through. Poor Emma. I've never seen anyone cry so much. She was inconsolable for a long, long time."

"I'm sure she was. A little girl needs her mother."

"The grief was just unbearable, Josie. For both of us. By the time I was able to lift my head out of the mire, I was drowning in medical debt, the restaurant was failing, and Emma..." He simply shook his head. "She was so sad. I tried to handle it all. I really did. But in the end, I botched up everything. I had to sell the restaurant in order to pay the doctors, the surgeon, the hospital. I was able to keep a roof over our heads, but that's about it."

The urge to wrap him in a consoling hug nearly overwhelmed her, and she reached down and curled her fingers over the edges of the seat of the chair to remain in place. What a nightmare he and Emma had experienced.

"I needed a job," he said. "One that would offer me pay year round. So I started going around to the restaurants that are open all year, but no one needed a chef. Then one night Deloris called me and asked me to come work here."

Here he paused, and he looked as though he was caught up in some memory.

Finally, he said, "You know, I almost turned her down." He exhaled a huff. "For a second, I actually felt insulted. I saw myself as a chef, not a short order cook." His brows pinched together and he murmured, "What an idiot I was, huh?"

Alex blinked and looked her in the eyes. "Deloris has been great. She pays me a good wage. She's understanding about Emma. And we work well together." He offered Josie a lopsided grin. "Except for when I'm calling 911. Then, she doesn't like me so much."

She just smiled in response. It made her feel warm inside to know that Grams had helped him out when he'd been in need. She also liked the idea of him being here watching out for her grandmother for the past couple of years.

"Speaking of working well together," he said. "I think you and I did a-okay today."

"You didn't think we would?"

He lifted his hands from his thighs. "Well, the way I figure it, things could have gone either way. We do have a bit of a past, remember."

A bit of a past? Is that how he thought of their one golden summer?

Josie let her gaze lower to a spot on the floor near the toes of her shoes. "If, as you said, Thursday is going to be busier than today, I pity my aching feet."

"I know just what you need."

Before Josie knew what was on his mind, he reached down and captured her ankle in his hand, bringing her heel up to rest on his knee.

"A little massage is in order, I'd say." He slid her shoe off her foot.

"Oh, no," she told him. "I can do that myself."

"You probably could."

The instant the pad of his thumb pressed against the center of the bottom of her foot, she closed her eyes and she exhaled slowly.

"But it just feels better when someone else does it," he said.

He ran both thumbs along the full length of her

foot, and she had to clamp her mouth closed to keep from moaning in pure pleasure. Even through her fine knit wool socks, his hands felt deliciously hot. Josie's muscles loosened.

Then he pressed his knuckles lightly into the ball of her foot and moved in tiny circles.

"That feels so good." She drew out the *so*, long and lazy.

When she finally opened her eyes, Alex was grinning at her as he continued to rub her foot. She'd never expected to see those sea green eyes looking at her like that ever again. Her heart thrummed a fluttery beat.

A sharp tapping on glass drew their attention to the front door. Emma waved from the other side. Alex stood up, and Josie's foot thumped to the floor.

He murmured an apology and went to let his daughter inside. Josie slid her foot into her shoe and followed him.

"Did I get here in time to set the tables?" Emma asked.

"You sure did," he told her. He looked at Josie. "On Sundays, she helps Deloris put fresh placemats on the tables so we're ready for Thursday service." Alex waved his thanks to the woman who'd dropped off his daughter and then re-engaged the bolt lock. He turned and put his hands on his hips, looking at Emma. "So did you have a good day?"

"I had a great day," she exclaimed. "Chloe's mom took us to all three outlets." Emma swung her attention to Josie. "Dad usually gets tired after shopping at one."

"Chloe's mom is an endurance athlete when it comes to shopping," Alex said in his defense. "I see you made some purchases."

"Yeah. Just a pair of jeans and some socks. And a fleece scarf that was eighty percent off." The child set down her bags. "Dad, Chloe's on the planning committee for the Valentine's Day dance at school. One of the kids had to drop out. Her parents are taking her to Walt Disney World that week so she won't be around to help set up and stuff. Chloe asked me if I could fill the spot."

Josie wondered if the girl planned to take a breath any time soon.

"We'll have to make posters," Emma continued without pause. "And plan some food. I think cupcakes would be nice. And maybe some soda. And Chloe says we have to organize a list of music and give it to Mr. O'Hannon next week. We also have to—"

"Whoa, whoa." Alex waved his hands in front of him. "Hold on a minute. This is the first I've heard about a dance."

"Well, it didn't seem all that exciting," Emma told him. "Until now. I get to help plan it."

"Okay. I still have some work left to do in the kitchen," he said. "Come on back there and let's talk."

Emma took a couple of steps and then stopped in her tracks. "Miss Josie, would you save me some tables to set?"

"I sure will."

Josie watched them amble toward the kitchen.

"So tell me all about it," Alex said.

Emma slipped her hand into her dad's. "I'll tell you *everything*."

The endearing sight of father and daughter made Josie smile.

Chapter Four

"That woman doesn't know what she's talking about. And even if she does, I will *not* eat oatmeal for breakfast."

"She's a trained dietitian," Josie gently reminded her grandmother for the second time. "Besides, what's wrong with oatmeal?"

When she'd arrived on this sunny Monday morning she'd hoped Grams would be in better humor than she'd been last night. The cardiologist had not made an appearance on Sunday, and that had put Grams in a sour mood. Josie had walked into the hospital room, toting a colorful helium balloon and a bright smile, but neither seemed to lift her grandmother's spirits.

"A little cinnamon," Josie offered breezily, "a

little brown sugar. It's delicious. And it's good for you."

Grams wrinkled her nose. "No amount of cinnamon and brown sugar will keep oatmeal from tasting like soggy cardboard to me."

"Oh, Grams, it's not that bad," she said softly. "You've got to do something about your diet."

"Listen to me." Grams caught Josie's hand. "I know it's hard for you young people to understand, but I grew up dirt poor. We had next to nothing. Oatmeal was all we had to eat for breakfast every single day. It was bland and boring, and I swore that, once I could afford better, I would never eat that stuff again." She tipped up her chin. "And that is one promise I intend to keep. So just put that in your pipe and smoke it."

At that moment, Alex and Emma walked into the room.

"But, Miss Deloris," Emma exclaimed, her eyes growing big as she slid her arms out of her coat, "there's no smoking in the hospital."

"It's just a saying," Grams told her. "There will be no smoking going on in here. I promise. Thanks for coming to see me. I needed a happy smile this morning."

"Hey!" Josie laughed. "What am I, Grams? A bowl of oatmeal?"

Emma and Alex both stared, perplexed.

"Don't mind her," Grams told them. "She's just being silly."

Alex let his leather jacket fall off his shoulders and he tossed it onto the wide window sill along with Emma's coat. Josie let her gaze rove over the cream colored sweater that hugged his broad chest. He looked firmly muscled without being overly brawny. His face was freshly-shaven and Josie was hit with the urge to lean closer and inhale the warm scent of him.

He met her gaze, pausing for a second, and then his mouth twitched with a knowing grin. Her pulse puttered as she veered her attention back to her grandmother.

"How are you feeling, Deloris?" he asked.

"I'm good." The elderly lady straightened her blanket. "In fact, if it wasn't for the cardiac catheterization they're talking about I'd get myself dressed and go on home."

"Grams," Josie said, "I told you not to worry about the procedure. I'll stay to help out in the diner for as long as you need me." Looking at Alex, she added, "According to the nurse, Grams should be up on her feet in just a few hours afterwards. And she'll probably get the okay to return to work after a week or so."

"Depending on what they do while they're in there," Grams groused.

Josie's tone lifted with optimism. "Maybe they won't have to do anything."

"If the dad-blamed cardiologist ever gets in here," Deloris said, "I might get some answers to my questions."

"Dad," Emma said, "I'm thirsty. Could I go find someplace to buy a juice or something?"

"But we just got here, sweetheart," Alex said.

The child slid her purse onto her shoulder. "You can stay."

Alex shook his head. "I don't want you wandering around the hospital by yourself."

"Oh, I don't want to go alone," Emma told him. "I was thinking maybe Josie would go with me."

"That's a good idea." Deloris looked up at Josie. "Do you mind? That way, Alex and I can... visit."

Alex's mouth twisted. "You're not still mad at me about calling 911, are you, Deloris?"

Josie watched Grams flap her hands. "Oh, I'm over that."

Grabbing the strap of her purse, Josie said, "Emma and I will be back in a bit."

"Thanks, Josie," Alex said.

Out in the hallway, Emma's brow wrinkled. "Don't be mad," she whispered, "but I'm not thirsty."

"Oh?"

"I saw your balloon," she said. "And I wanted to get Miss Deloris a present. Can we go to the gift shop?"

"Aw, that's sweet," Josie told her. "You don't have to spend—"

"I want to," Emma blurted. "Miss Deloris is like a grandmom to me. Both sets of my grandparents live far away. Pop-pop and Mom-mom Thompson moved to Savannah. Mom's parents drive a big RV around the country. I don't see them very often. Miss Deloris is... well, she's kinda special."

Josie smiled. "I think she's special, too."

They stepped onto the elevator, and as they rode down toward the lobby, Emma said, "You're really pretty, Josie."

"Well, thank you."

"Daddy thinks so, too," she added.

Surprise had Josie floundering for words. The

elevator doors slid open and they stepped out into the vestibule.

"I asked him," Emma said rather bluntly. Then she offered a shrug. "If you want to know something, ya gotta ask, right?"

"You're right about that." Josie's voice went soft.

"Sometimes daddy gets annoyed and says I ask too many questions. But he didn't snap at me or anything when I asked him if he thought you were pretty."

Again, Josie felt at a loss as to how to respond. Luckily, she didn't have to because Emma changed the subject.

"I think it's really nice of you to help at the diner until Miss Deloris gets better. Daddy said he's glad you're here to help out."

They entered the hospital's gift shop and Emma made a beeline for the stuffed animals.

"Do you think Miss Deloris would like a walrus?" She giggled. "I love his tusks, don't you?"

Before Josie could answer, Emma set the stuffed walrus back on the shelf.

"Where do you live?" she asked Josie.

"I have an apartment about three hours away. In Rockville."

Emma slid her fingers down the white fur of a

tiny unicorn. "Three hours. That's a long way, huh?"

"About a hundred and sixty miles."

"You got a husband in Rockville?"

"No."

The girl picked up a small sock monkey. "Ah, so you're divorced?"

Josie shook her head. "Nope."

Emma frowned. "You got a boyfriend?"

"No." Rather than becoming annoyed at the grilling, Josie actually wanted to laugh.

"So... how come?" Emma studied the monkey as she arranged it next to the unicorn.

"How come what?"

Her little shoulders lifted in a shrug. "How come you never got married? How come you don't have a boyfriend?"

"I guess you could say those opportunities never presented themselves."

"I can't believe that."

The lack of guile in the child's voice made Josie chuckle.

"Not everyone gets married, Emma."

"I think I'll get the unicorn," she announced, plucking the white animal from the shelf. "It'll keep Miss Deloris company at night when no one is around."

"Good choice."

Emma rooted around in her purse. "Josie, what if Miss Deloris needs you for longer than a week? Would you stay in Ocean City?"

"Of course. Like I told her, I'll stay as long as she needs me."

"Would you stay for, say, two weeks?"

Josie stopped and looked at Emma as she continued to search in her purse.

"Emma, why do I get the feeling you have a hidden agenda?"

The child looked into Josie's face. "What's a hidden agenda?"

"An ulterior motive." But the phrase didn't help Emma one bit, so Josie tried again. "Um, your questions about my staying don't have as much to do with my grandmother as you're making out. Am I right?"

Emma blinked and then sighed. "Yeah, I guess you're right." She pulled several bills from her purse. "Josie, do you like my dad?"

Ah, the final piece of the puzzle.

"Emma, are you trying to play matchmaker?"

The child's head tipped to the side and she gazed

at the unicorn. "Well, I'm not trying to marry you off, if that's what you mean. I'd just like for my dad to go on a date. He's been out of circulation too long."

Out of circulation? Alex had told Josie his daughter was *twelve going on twenty-nine.* His assessment was right on target.

"All he has is cooking at the diner," Emma said. "And me. He needs more than just a job and a kid."

Josie licked her lips, not trusting herself to respond to such sophisticated insight coming from a child.

"Right before school started, Chloe's parents split up," Emma told her. "I thought it would be cool if dad asked Chloe's mom to go out to dinner. But he didn't think it was a good idea. I tried to change his mind for days, and then, *bam*, Chloe told me her mom found a boyfriend. Dad's chance was gone."

The idea of explaining the ins and outs of dating to this child scared Josie witless. And she was almost one hundred percent certain that Alex wouldn't want her to attempt it. But something niggled at the back of Josie's mind. She crossed her arms and dipped her chin. "Emma, hon, I have to ask you something. What's with the two weeks you mentioned? A date takes one night."

"Are you kidding me?" The girl tucked her wallet back into her purse and closed the leather flap. "It'll take me two weeks to get him to believe the idea is his. Dad is really slow when it comes to some things. And if he even suspects I'm trying to tell him what to do, he'll go berserk."

"Wait..." But the rest of Josie's thought faded into oblivion. How had this half-pint child come up with such tricky ideas when it came to her father?

Emma lowered her voice. "Don't you see? I have to make this happen. Because when it comes to women and dating my dad is really out of practice." She planted a hand on her little hip. "Actually, he's hopeless. But if I have some time, I can probably make it happen."

Poor Alex didn't have a chance.

Chapter Five

"**S**he said that? That she needed to make me think it was my idea?" Alex stopped mincing the red peppers on the cutting board and looked across the diner's kitchen at Josie, incredulity brightening his green gaze.

Commiseration pulled at her features as she nodded.

Both Alex and Josie were taking advantage of Thursday's mid-morning lull. He was prepping vegetables he'd need during the lunch rush, and she was putting away the food order that had been delivered just a few minutes ago.

Josie had thought long and hard about whether to tell him about her conversation with Emma at the hospital on Monday. All she'd had to do to decide to tell him was to imagine herself in his shoes. He was Emma's dad; he deserved to know that his daughter was plotting a scheme. She'd been forced to wait three days, however, because she'd been so busy with Grams. The cardiac catheterization had been performed on Tuesday, and the single blockage found in her grandmother's heart had been opened with angioplasty and a single stent. Yesterday, Josie had brought her grandmother home and gotten her settled in her apartment upstairs where Deloris had strict orders from the doctor to rest for at least a week.

This was the first opportunity Josie had to talk to Alex about Emma.

"You just wait until she gets home from school." The knife Alex wielded made solid thumping sounds against the board. "I'm going to talk to her about her manipulating ways."

Josie shoved the block of cheese onto the shelf and slammed shut the refrigerator. "Oh, no." She whirled around. "You can't do that. She'll know I told you."

"But I can't let her think she can pull my strings and make me dance like a puppet." He waved the knife in the air.

"Look, all she wants you to do is go on a date." Josie lifted her hands, palms up, and shrugged. "The answer seems simple enough. Just go out on a date."

He went still, his eyes narrowing just a smidge.

Realizing the implication behind her suggestion, she felt her face flame and she backed up a half step. "Wait. I wasn't saying—I don't mean to suggest you should go out with *me*. I'm saying you should call one of your lady friends and take her out to dinner. Simple solution."

"I don't have any lady friends," he muttered. "Besides, how would that be a solution? I'd be doing exactly what she wants me to do."

"But she wouldn't be making it happen," Josie quickly explained. "It needs to look like it's your idea before she even gets involved. That would make the situation reverse, reverse psychology." Uncertain if any of what she was saying made sense, she added, "Of sorts."

"Reverse, reverse manipulation, you mean." He set down the knife. "Where did Emma get the idea that she's supposed to control me?"

"Women battling for control? Oh, I don't know," Josie said, busying herself with stocking the shelf with large cans of tuna. "Does she watch prime time TV? How about commercials? Does she go to the movie theater? Or how about—"

"Okay, okay. I get it." Alex scooped up the chopped peppers and deposited them into a stainless steel container.

She set the empty plastic packing crate by the back door, and when she returned, she said, "You should know, Alex, her heart is in the right place."

The bell hanging on the front door jangled, keeping her from further explanation.

"Customer," Josie murmured, automatically dipping into the pocket of her apron for the pad and pencil she used to jot down orders. "I'll get them seated."

"Hey, wait."

She turned and watched as Alex dried his hands and tossed the towel on the stainless steel island. He took the three steps that separated them and he gazed into her face with those beautiful green eyes of his. Josie clutched the tiny pad.

"So will you do it?" he asked her, softly. "Will you go out on a *date* with me?" He placed air quotes around the word.

When she didn't answer right away his eyebrows arched. "Hey, this was your idea, remember."

She winced. "I remember." Still, she hesitated to agree.

"How about Monday night? I could pick you up at seven. I'll bring Emma so she can keep Deloris company while we're gone. I'll leave the apron at home. I'll shower. I'll wear street clothes. I won't smell like garlic and onions." He grinned at her, reaching out and tucking a strand of her hair behind her ear. "I promise."

This wasn't a good idea. Josie could feel it in her gut. She worried her upper lip between her teeth, reminding herself she was no longer the teen who had harbored a crush on the cutest boy in town. She was an adult who was completely in control of her emotions.

"Okay." She nodded. "Monday night it is."

She'd be fine, she told herself. Just fine.

Chapter Six

The Sunday afternoon lunch service had been so dead that Alex and Josie decided to work on a heart-healthy recipe that Deloris would not only enjoy enough to incorporate into her own diet, but also one she might consider adding to the diner's menu. The resulting vegetarian chili and jalapeño corn muffins that Alex had made filled the kitchen with a scrumptious aroma.

"Here, try this."

Alex dipped a spoon into the pot and held it out for her to taste. Josie leaned forward. His free hand hovered beneath the spoon to catch any drips, and just when her lips touched the chili-laced diced vegetables and beans, his fingers grazed the underside of her chin. A delicious jolt skittered through her and she straightened her spine.

"Mmmm, that's so good," she told him. "It's really rich. And there's a lot going on with the spices. It's got... I don't know. Depth. There's more than just chili powder in there, isn't there?"

"Chili powder, fresh garlic, a pinch of oregano, cumin, smoked paprika, a tiny bit of cinnamon—"

"Cinnamon? It's really good, Alex."

Since they'd talked about Emma and had set up their dinner date, something had shifted in their relationship. The air felt easier, less businesslike, and more genial. And they laughed. A lot. Josie enjoyed the change. She felt she could relax a little.

"Do you think you can sell Deloris on all these vegetables?"

"I have no idea." She held out a glass bowl for him to fill. "But I promise to give it my all. Her doctor really wants her to change her diet." Josie snapped a lid onto the bowl and then wrapped up two muffins in aluminum foil to keep them warm until she could get upstairs. She picked up the food and said, "Wish me luck."

"You're going to need it," he told her.

Josie went outside, rounded the corner of the building and raced up the steps leading to the upstairs apartment. She let herself in and called out, "Grams, I brought lunch."

"I'm in the kitchen."

"What are you doing?" Josie hurried through the living room and entered the kitchen.

Grams stood near the pantry, a can of soup in her hand.

"I told you I was going to bring you something to eat." Josie set the food on the table and took off her coat.

"I was hungry."

"Well, food is here now." Josie pulled open a drawer and plucked out a spoon. "Sit. This is special. Alex made it just for you."

"Oh, Lord, save me," Grams groan. "It's not one of those nasty spinach smoothie things I've heard about, is it?"

Josie laughed. "Nothing as bad as that. Surely, you smell the spices. Chili and cumin. I want you to keep an open mind, okay?"

Grams slid into a chair at the table, warning, "I'm an old dog, Josie."

"You're going to love this. It's delicious." As she spoke, she grabbed a bowl, a small plate, the butter dish, setting them in front of her grandmother.

"It does smell good, I'll give you that."

"Can't find more homey food than chili and cornbread, right?"

Grams eyed the chili, then she picked up her spoon and moved the vegetables around. Keeping her gaze focused on the bowl, she asked, "Where's the beef?"

"It's veggie chili. No animal fat to clog your arteries. Don't think about it. Just taste it."

Lifting a spoonful, Grams remarked, "It is colorful." She took a bite and chewed.

Josie got up and pulled a spoon from the cutlery drawer for herself. "So, what do you think?"

"It's tasty." She set the spoon down. "But I can't lie, Josie. I miss the ground beef."

"Try the corn muffin. Alex swapped out the bacon grease in your recipe—"

"No bacon grease?"

Clearly, Grams thought this was sacrilege. Her grandmother tipped up her chin and looked down her nose at the muffin.

"It'll be dry as an old bone."

"It's not," Josie assured her. "Alex used olive oil instead. It's a healthier fat."

Grams picked it up, broke it in half, and sniffed it. "It smells smoky. But there's no bacon grease?"

"Alex used a splash of liquid smoke. Try it. It's really good. I promise."

She bit and chewed and swallowed. "Is that minced jalapeños in there?" Then she nodded. "I'd eat that."

Josie's smile went wide. "Alex and I would like to put the chili and muffins on the menu this week. What do you think? We can call them Heart Healthy. Or Fresh and Wholesome. I don't know. We'll come up with something."

"That's not going to work," Grams said. "People don't come to the diner looking for health food. They want good, ol' fashioned comfort food."

"Comfort food doesn't have to be full of saturated fat, Grams. You serve enough bacon to give everyone in town heart disease."

"There's a reason for that. Bacon makes everything taste better." Grams took another bite of the chili. "And I'm sure you're overstating the facts about my detrimental effect on the health of my friends and neighbors."

"Only a little." Josie grinned as she dipped her spoon into the bowl she'd carried upstairs. "Mmm. Alex did a good job. It's really delicious."

"It is good," Grams admitted, then she went quiet so she could chew. "You know, back in summer I had quite a few young people come into the diner asking if we were vegan friendly. All I had to offer them was green salads. Maybe we could add something like this to the menu during the summer months. Chili won't work in the hot months, of course. But something else. Roasted vegetables, maybe, served over some sort of fancy rice or couscous or quinoa. I'll talk to Alex." She scooped up another spoonful. "But it's off season, and I know my regulars. I just don't think they'll order this, Josie. But I don't want to be a nay-sayer. Add the chili to the menu this week. See if they go for it." She broke off a piece of muffin and popped it into her mouth.

Josie sat back and stared at Grams in silence.

"What?" her grandmother asked.

"I'm so proud of you." Josie rested her hands on her thighs. "Never in a million years would I have guessed that you'd be so open minded about this."

"What can I say?" Grams lifted her shoulders. "The years have worn off my sharp angles."

"Some of them, maybe." Josie picked up her spoon. As she was enjoying the chili, she happened to glance up and see the card propped up on the counter.

"Someone sent you a get well card?" she asked Grams.

"It's from Peg."

"Mom sent a card?" Utter amazement embellished the question like fancy fringe.

"Yeah, I know," Grams said. "I felt the same way."

Josie reached for the card, read the message, and then looked at her grandmother.

"I always suspected," Josie said, "that you and Mom didn't get along because of me."

"What? Why would you think such a thing?"

"Mom got pregnant with me," she continued, "and she refused to get married to Jerry Higgins."

Josie had never referred to Jerry Higgins as her father or her dad. No one else had, either. And no one ever called him just Jerry. He was always called Jerry Higgins. That might have been different if Jerry Higgins had hung around long enough to meet his daughter. But he hadn't.

"Granted," Grams said, "I thought your mom should marry the father of her child. But your mom thought that was an old fashioned way of thinking." She looked across the table. "But you, sweet Jojo, had nothing to do with the ill feelings between your mom and me."

"So if it wasn't me, what was it?"

Her grandmother pressed her palm to her wrinkled cheek. "Oh, honey, I wish I knew. It's just years and years of... stuff. If I were to tell you what I would do in any given situation, Peg would do the exact opposite every single time. We were just never on the same page. With anything."

Josie nodded, knowing from great experience that making sound decisions was not a trait her mother possessed.

"So how are things in the diner?" Grams asked. "Are you and Alex able to work together? You getting along okay?"

The mention of Alex made her go all warm, sweet, and gooey inside, like hot caramel sauce. "We're good, Grams."

Now it was her grandmother's turn to stare. After a moment, she said, "Okay, Josie, so what's going on?"

"Going on?" Josie focused too much attention on the bowl sitting in the center of the table. "Nothing's going on."

"Okay."

"We're running the diner, Grams. Just like you wanted."

"I said okay."

When Josie dared to look across the table, she saw a gleam in her grandmother's eyes.

* * *

Suspecting that Alex had locked the diner's front door, Josie pushed her way into the kitchen from the rear of the building. A burst of cold air rolled in along with her.

Alex was bent over the stainless steel island, emptying leftovers into air-tight containers.

"I can't believe it," Josie blurted, hanging her coat on the hook by the door. "She liked it. The chili, the corn muffins, and the idea to add both to the menu."

"Whoa. I've got to admit, that's a surprise." After snapping the lid on a plastic container, he turned and set the empty bowl in the sink. "I fully expected you to come back here with your tail tucked and your bottom lip dragging. Further proof of your powers of persuasion."

"I'm shocked." She told him what Grams had said about developing some vegan items for the summer menu.

"Sounds good. I'll make a fresh pot of chili on Thursday morning and we'll see if we can sell it."

"Alex," she said, and she waited until he looked

at her. "I'm worried. I think maybe Grams is afraid. I didn't think she'd even try your chili, but..."

He reached across the island and covered her hand with his. "Focus on the good part. Yeah, the heart attack probably did scare her. But she's shown you that she's trying to get better and do better."

His thumb stroked across the back of her hand, and Josie happily accepted the comfort he offered.

She smiled. "So you're suggesting she's been scared straight?"

He chuckled and straightened. "That's what it looks like to me." He shook open a brown paper bag. "Listen, Deloris and I usually split the leftovers. You take the rest of the chili upstairs when you go. But the tuna salad and egg salad won't keep until Thursday, and there's mayo in both of them. Deloris is probably not supposed to have it. So I thought I'd drop it off at the homeless shelter on my way home, if that's okay."

"I think that's a great idea."

The phone on the wall rang and Josie started toward it.

"There might be something wrong with the phone line," Alex said. "I've answered it twice, but I don't think the caller could hear me."

Josie picked up the receiver. "Joe's Place. How can I help you?"

"Josie," Emma said, her voice a frantic whisper, "please don't say my name. I don't want my dad to know it's me."

Startled by the request, Josie turned her back on Alex and said, "Hi!" Immediately, she worried that she'd put too much ebullience in the greeting. More calmly, she asked, "Are you okay?"

"No," Emma said. "Can you come?"

"Where are you?"

"At home. There's blood, Josie. Don't tell Dad! It's... it's... the first time I did this." Emma's voice went low. "It's a... a girl thing."

Blood and a *girl thing*. Okay. Josie nodded. She could handle this.

"Give me your address, hon," she said. "Relax. It's going to be all right. This happens to every woman in the world. I'll be right there."

Josie hung up the phone and turned to face the heart of the kitchen. "Alex, I have to go out," she said. "A friend has an emergency."

He looked up at her, concern drawing his brows together. "Everything okay?"

"Everything's fine. Just going to go lend some moral support." She grabbed her coat and purse.

"I'll come back later and take care of the dining room."

"Okay. See you tomorrow night."

He smiled, and Josie felt a little pinch of guilt as she nodded. She should probably tell him about Emma. What his daughter was experiencing was completely normal and natural. But Emma had sounded mortified by the idea of her father knowing, so Josie thought it best to just go help her out and let her Emma tell Alex about it when she was ready.

After a quick stop at a pharmacy where she picked up several different brands of tampons and pads, Josie headed to the north end of town. Just a few minutes later, she parked in the driveway, hurried up the walk, and rang the bell.

Emma answered the door, her eyes moist with tears, the left leg of her leggings shoved up to her thigh, and an angry cut on her knee welling with fresh blood. "It won't stop bleeding! Do I need stitches?"

Josie dropped the bag of feminine products and slid out of her coat, letting it fall to the floor in a heap by the door. "What did you do, sweetie? Let's go get you cleaned up."

"I didn't come to the diner to help out today

because Chloe came over." Emma headed down the hallway with Josie close on her heels. "We were making posters for the Valentine's Day dance. She told me she got a new dress. And then she started talking about how she'd shaved her legs. It sounded cool, getting rid of this ugly, dark hair, so I thought I'd give it a try."

Emma entered the bathroom, used the toilet seat to climb up onto the countertop, and sat so that her leg was propped over the sink. Josie saw red circles staining the white porcelain bowl. An open package of disposable razors sat nearby.

Blood dripped down the side of Emma's knee and she patted at it with a tissue.

"What you need," Josie said, taking the wad of tissue and tossing it into the trash can, "is steady pressure. No more dabbing. You keep disturbing the raw edges and the blood can't clot. Do you have any gauze?" She opened the medicine cabinet and found everything she needed to clean and treat the cut.

"You can't shave dry skin," Josie offered, applying a bit of antibiotic ointment before covering the cut tightly with folded gauze and a bandage.

"I've watched daddy shave." Emma reached

behind her and held up a can. "I know I need shaving cream. But I was just getting started. I was holding the razor and I scooted closer to the sink. It happened so fast, I don't even remember the razor touching my knee."

"Yeah." Josie flattened her mouth and shook her head. "Razors demand a great deal of respect, that's for sure. You have to really focus on what you're doing. Especially when you're first learning how."

Emma popped the lid off the shaving cream.

"Whoa. Wait." Josie plucked the can from the girl's hand. "What are you doing?"

"I'm going to shave my legs."

"Hon, you should wait until that cut heals."

Instantly, stubbornness tightened her features. "It took me two whole hours to get up the courage to do this. I'm doing it." Then she swallowed and asked, "Will you stay?"

Josie thought back to when she'd first started shaving her legs and underarms. She couldn't remember exactly how old she'd been, but she did remember the teasing she'd suffered from her middle school peers that made her decide to lock herself in the bathroom and borrow her mother's razor without asking. Her poor knees and ankles had seen many a nick and gash before she'd become proficient at the job.

"Okay, how about if I show you?" Josie took off her shoe and sock. Then she rolled up the leg of her jean to above her knee. "Don't touch the razor until you're ready to actually use it. Turn on the hot water so it just trickles and dampen all the skin you want to shave. One leg at a time, of course. Now, you can certainly use the shaving cream, but it smells... well, kind of manly, don't you think?" She twisted to look inside the tub and plucked up a plastic bottle she found there, offering it to Emma. "Here's what I use. Hair conditioner will allow the razor to glide really easily, and it has moisturizers that will leave your skin feeling nice and soft."

"Cool," Emma said. "I can't wait to tell Chloe about this trick. She said she uses soap."

While Emma smoothed the creamy conditioner over her shin and calf, Josie offered some tips. "Always inspect your razor before you start." She propped her bare foot up on the toilet seat. "These are new, but just remember to never use a rusty blade, and if the metal looks bent or the plastic looks damaged, throw it away. When you feel the blade pulling, it means the razor is dull and you need a new one."

Emma nodded her understanding.

Josie applied conditioner to her own skin and then took a razor from the package. "You want to bend your leg, just as you're doing, so you can reach your ankles. Start at your ankle and draw the blade up your leg in a slow, straight stroke. Don't go too fast and never move the razor sideways." She finished running the razor up her own shin and then looked at Emma. "Now you try."

Emma looked as nervous as Josie felt.

"Easy," Josie said softly. "Good. Good. Now rinse the razor. Keep the blade nice and clean." Josie held her razor under the running water. "Now let's try it again. Be very careful shaving your knee. It's easy to nick the edges of your knee cap."

"What is going on here?"

Alex's deep voice startled both Josie and Emma.

"Alex!" Josie planted her one bare foot on the floor. "Never sneak up on a woman when she's holding a razor."

"Dad, you scared us to death." Emma reached down and turned off the faucet.

His gaze trailed the length of Josie's ankle, leg, and torso, finally letting it come to rest on her face. "So this is the emergency you told me about?"

Josie blinked. His tone sounded calm enough, but his jaw looked tense.

"Dad, don't be mad," Emma piped up, "I called her because I cut myself. It was an accident, and she helped me. I'm old enough to shave my legs. Chloe's mom lets her do it. All the other girls at school are doing it, too. Chloe said so. Josie was just showing me how. So I wouldn't cut my whole knee off."

Josie listened as the child covered all her bases with the perfect amount of pre-teen melodrama.

Alex looked at his daughter. "You called the diner and hung up on me twice."

Emma blanched, her confidence waning. "Sometimes you just need to talk to another girl."

He sighed and reached around to scrub the back of his neck with his palm. "I'll be in the kitchen, heating up some mugs of apple cider. We need to talk about the way this went down, young lady."

"Yes, sir," Emma said. "We'll be out just as soon as I finish my other leg."

He heaved another sigh. And then he cleared his throat. Josie and Emma both looked at him.

"So, ah, Josie," he said, "we still on for dinner tomorrow night?"

Instantly, Josie realized the question was solely for his daughter's benefit.

"Sure," Josie said. She figured she should smile, but the awkwardness pervading the suddenly too small bathroom prevented it.

Alex looked at Emma. "Would you keep Deloris company while Josie and I go out to dinner?"

"I can do that." The girl's eyes had grown large.

He stuffed his hands into his pockets, offered a silent nod, and then disappeared from the doorway.

Emma drew in a slow, shocked inhalation. She whispered, "Daddy asked you to go out?"

A dry wash cloth sat on the counter. Josie picked it up and started wiping the conditioner residue from her calf. "Yeah. A couple of days ago."

Awe softened Emma's tone as she asked, "Why didn't you tell me?"

Josie lifted her gaze. "It went right out of my head the instant I saw that you'd nearly cut your whole knee off."

Emma's serious expression dissolved and she giggled, and the delighted sound of it made Josie laugh, too.

After supervising the leg-shaving operation to the end, Josie left Emma alone to shower and she went to look for Alex. She followed the scent of warm apple cider and found him pulling a mug from the microwave.

"Alex, I'm sorry if I overstepped the bounds."

He turned and silently invited her into the room by holding out the cider. Josie went to him and took the mug, her fingers brushing his in the process. Something akin to crackling static coursed across her skin.

"What's with all that, um, female paraphernalia by the front door?" he asked.

Josie tipped her head back. "Oh, I forgot all about that. When Emma called, I misunderstood what she meant when she said her problem was '*a girl thing*.'"

"Ah." Then he looked pained. "Is she ready for it? All that stuff, I mean? Has she, you know... started?"

Lifting her shoulders, Josie shook her head. "I don't know. I walked into the house, saw the cut on her knee, and I forgot all about it."

"A father should know that kind of thing, shouldn't he?"

Josie rested the warm mug against the palm of her hand. "Alex, relax. If Emma had started having her period, I think you would know. Just store that stuff under the bathroom sink and you'll be ready when she does need it."

"You're right. Thanks. I guess it's time Emma and I had a serious talk." He moved closer and slid his hands along Josie's forearms, cupping her elbows in the palms of his hands. "I don't know how I feel about my little girl shaving her legs, but I do want you to know I'm grateful that you came when she called. You dropped everything and you came to help her. It means a lot to me."

The air between them went still and a silky intimacy wrapped around them.

"I was happy to do it." The words sounded breathy to Josie's ears.

He reached up and traced his fingers along her jaw, and she let her eyes flutter shut so she could enjoy the feel of it.

"I'll be out in one minute!" Emma called from the back of the house.

Alex took a backward step and his hands dropped away from Josie, almost as if touching her was some sort of wrongful act.

"Heat up my cider, would ya, Dad?"

He turned toward the microwave and called, "I'm on it."

Josie set the mug on the counter. "I think I'm going to go so you and Emma can talk."

"You're sure you don't want to finish your cider?"

She looked into his eyes, but the cozy feeling that she'd sensed just a moment before was gone, and she was left wondering if she'd imagined it.

"I should really go," Josie told him. "Don't be too hard on her. I was right around her age when I started shaving." Josie lifted one shoulder. "It's just a part of growing up."

Alex nodded. "Thanks again," he said.

She smiled and then headed for the front door.

Chapter Seven

The sky was dark, the air calm and cold, when Josie and Alex got into his car on Monday evening. He turned the ignition key, and after a single rev, the engine purred.

"Let me get some heat going," he said, fiddling with the controls at the center of the dashboard.

Josie secured her seatbelt with a click.

"We have some time before our reservation." His leather jacket scrunched against the seat when he shifted his weight. "Do you mind if we make a stop?"

"That's fine. Where're we going?"

Alex put the car in gear. "You'll see."

Josie had battled the giddiness in her belly all day long. Even though this "date" was nothing more than a setup for Emma's sake, Josie still felt nervous about going out with Alex. Working together at the diner, they had a job to focus on all day long, chores and customers that kept them busy. But tonight it would be just the two of them. She'd kept telling herself that there was no possibility of them talking about the past; he would be just as eager to avoid the subject as she was. They'd order dinner, they'd talk about Joe's Place, new items for the menu, Emma and the great leg shaving caper; they'd even talk about Deloris. And then he'd take her home. It would all be over in just a couple of hours.

The quiet in the car made her antsy, so she said, "Grams was really surprised when I told her you'd asked me to dinner. I wasn't sure you'd want her to know that we were... um..."

"Pulling some reverse, reverse psychology on Emma?" He chuckled.

Josie let her eyes slide shut for just a moment and imagined placing her palm on his chest so she could feel the vibration of his laugh. Heat pumped out of the vents, and the scent of his cologne swathed her in hints of citrus and cedar. He smelled delicious. Shadowy tendrils curled low in her gut, and the instant Josie recognized the desire for what it was, she opened her eyes and took in a slow, calming breath.

"I'm still not sure I'm doing the right thing," he said. "But we've started it now, so let's just try to enjoy ourselves."

Not trusting herself to speak, she merely smiled when he glanced her way.

"Here we are," he murmured.

He turned onto a side street that led to the beach, passing all the empty parking slots, and drove the car up onto the wide, hard-packed ramp on the sand dune. He stopped at the top and put the gearshift into Park.

"I saw there's a full moon tonight," Alex said. "I couldn't wait to bring you here. What does this remind you of?"

The fat, white moon hung over the inky black water, glittering like gems on the frothy tops of a thousand choppy waves. It was breathtaking. A truly magical sight. And Josie hadn't realized just how much she'd missed seeing it until this very moment.

"Isn't it romantic?" he asked, his tone whisper soft.

"Alex." His name seemed to grate in her throat.

"I have to tell you," he continued, "I've thought

about bringing you here since the very first day we worked together in the diner. I saw you at the hospital that first night, and the memories of that summer just flooded my mind and wouldn't let me be."

She sensed him look over at her, but she kept her eyes on the onyx-colored ocean. Then he frowned; she sensed that, too.

"Please tell me you didn't forget."

She paused long enough to blink slowly twice, and she used the time to rein in the chaos of her thoughts. Talking about their past wasn't something she'd prepared herself to do. Finally, she swiveled her head and met his gaze.

"No," she whispered. Then louder, she added, "I didn't forget. I remember... everything."

Her answer satisfied him.

He clenched his fist and pressed it to his chest. "Oh, how you broke my heart."

Josie sat up a little straighter. "*I* broke *your* heart? Hold on just a minute, there. That's not how I remember it."

"What I meant to say, is that I was crushed by the whole situation."

"Hmmm," she breathed, unconvinced. "You

were so crushed you went out and got married just a few months later."

It was probably a mean-spirited thing to say, but Josie couldn't help herself.

He looked out the windshield toward the beach. "I was trying to do the right thing, and now I—"

"The right thing? Are you serious?" Josie heard the annoyance in her voice, and suddenly she felt she was reverting to her sixteen year old self whose heart had been ripped to shreds all those years ago. However, the past wasn't where she wanted to be, so she shoved her way out of it. "Look, we were kids who spent a few weeks necking on the beach—"

"And in the park," he said. "And on the boardwalk. And in the movie theater."

Her mouth twisted. She couldn't deny the truth. She'd loved kissing him. She'd loved holding his hand, walking on the boardwalk, the sand, the fishing pier. Loved being in his arms. Talking to him. Dreaming with him. He made her feel as if she'd stepped out of adolescence and into the world of adulthood. As sappy as that sounded, Josie knew it to be true even after all this time.

"But it was more than that," he told her, as if reading her mind. "And you know it. It wasn't just a few weeks. It was almost three months. It was a long and wonderful summer. And we got to know each other, Josie. You can't deny that. We talked about everything. No subject was off limits. I'd never experienced anything like that before with a girl. You told me about how difficult your life was. About how your mom struggled to earn enough money. About how your mom and your grandmother always fought. That your grandmother was disappointed that your mother never married your father. And I told you about my hopes and my dreams. My aspirations to earn a business degree, to someday start a business of my own." He shook his head. "What a joke that turned out to be."

"You remember all that stuff we talked about?"

"Of course, I remember. You don't?"

She pressed her mouth flat for a second. "No, I do. But it was all a long time ago, Alex." It was the only thing she could think of to say. Then for some unknown reason she blurted, "It was meaningless. Really. And I don't think we need to talk about it anymore."

The need to flee forced her out of the car and she walked further out onto the dune crossing. The damp, frosty air chilled her face and ears, and she stuffed her hands deep into her coat pockets. A million stars sparkled like bits of silver against black silk. She heard Alex open his door, but she didn't turn around.

He sidled up beside her and slipped his arm around her shoulders.

"I won't let you say it was meaningless," he said. "I feel guilty about how it ended, and I wish you'd let me explain."

She sighed and lightly rocked back on her heels. He wasn't going to let this go.

"There's nothing to explain." She kept her tone gentle. "The last night we were together, I told you I wasn't ready to go all the way, and I never saw you again. It's no big deal."

He shifted then, placing his hands on her arms and turning her to face him.

"Your not wanting to have sex," he told her, "is *not* why I took the job on the fishing boat for the last two weeks of that summer, Josie."

Skepticism had her pressing her lips together.

"When I went home that night," he said, "my gut was churning with emotions I'd never grappled with before. I was due to leave for college in Florida in just a couple of weeks, but my heart ached at the thought of moving so far away and not being able to see you."

The memory of the experience had him frowning.

"I told my mother I wanted to transfer to the University of Maryland." Lost in the past, he dipped his gaze toward the ground. "I figured that College Park wasn't so far from Rockville... from you. Then I made the mistake of asking her what it felt like to be in love. Because, for me, you were *it*, Josie."

His gaze locked onto her and she couldn't look away.

"I'd never experienced anything like that," he told her. "It was powerful and breathtaking, and I wanted to feel it for the rest of my life."

The earnestness in his words struck her.

"I was young, and very aware of my inexperience with girls. But what I felt was... life changing." His exhalation condensed into a white haze. "My parents realized that too, I think. And while my inclination back then was to stay as close to you as I could, *their* solution was to keep the two of us apart. Both of them used every argument they could think of. I was too young to become so serious about a girl. I was going to ruin my life. I was too old to be in a relationship with someone still in high school. They didn't need Deloris Baxter showing up on their doorstep, accusing me of taking advantage of her granddaughter. I needed to focus on my education if I wanted to get anywhere in life. It went on and on, for hours."

His fingers slid down her arms, and he took her hands in his.

"They were my parents," he said. "They'd never steered me wrong before. I'd never seen them so distraught about anything. I wanted to make them happy. Take away their worry."

"That's understandable, Alex."

"It's important to me that you know it was you I wanted."

He lifted her hand, pressed his soft, heated lips to the backs of her fingers. The hard crust around Josie's heart went soft and supple.

"Their arguments only half convinced me," he continued. "I agreed to take a job on a fishing boat owned by a friend of Dad's. Four o'clock the next morning, I was geared up, on board, and heading out into the Atlantic for two weeks. And I was heartsick every single day."

A smile tugged at Josie's mouth. "I know this isn't going to sound very nice, but I'm glad to hear it. Because I was heartsick, too. I spent the last two weeks of my summer vacation looking for you. Every day, I visited all the places we hung out. I rode the bus from the north end of town to the inlet. I even went to your house. All your father would say is that you weren't there." Josie moistened her lips. "I wish you'd have at least contacted me. I wish you'd have asked me how I felt about it."

"Oh, honey," he murmured. "I wanted to. My mom said that wouldn't be fair. She pointed out that I'd had the chance to enjoy my high school years, free and unfettered, and that you deserved that same experience." He shook his head ruefully. "It felt right to me at the time."

Finally, Josie sighed. "As I stand here looking back on it, I can't help but understand that your parents were just trying to do what they thought was best for you. And you wanted to make them proud."

Even though the moon cast shadows across his handsome face, Josie saw regret pull at his features.

"I did," he said, his tone a husky whisper. "But I screwed that up really quickly. I was home from the fishing trip only a matter of hours before I was packing my things into the car and driving off to

Florida State. I was confused, hurting, frustrated, and hellishly lonely. All I wanted to do was call you, see you, but I kept remembering my mom's words, insisting that you needed the space just as much as I did, and that I should be man enough to give you that space. She promised I'd meet other girls at uni."

He barked out a humorless laugh. "But I just wasn't interested. I spent the first three months at college with my head buried in books. I met Carin in a study group. She started pestering me about why I was so gloomy. She was funny and interesting and smart, and she was relentless in her determination to, I don't know, bring a little light into my world."

He blinked, but his gaze remained steadfastly fixed on Josie's as he admitted, "I finally surrendered."

His thumbs roved over the backs of her hands. "It couldn't have been but a few weeks later when she realized she was pregnant. What could we do? No, we weren't in love. But we liked each other well enough. And we were bringing a baby into the world." He shrugged. "So we got married. We both packed up and came home to Ocean City. I got work as a prep chef and found out pretty quick that I had a knack for cooking. I advanced to being a sous chef, and before I knew it, I was managing my own kitchen crew, creating my own menus. Carin and I scrimped and saved, and we opened a restaurant together. I wouldn't have been able to do it without her. Our marriage didn't start out as it probably should have, but we were a good team. And in the end, I loved her, Josie. I did. Sweet Emma was the light of our lives. When Carin got sick, I feared I wouldn't be able to make it without her."

His grief was palpable, and Josie slid her hands out of his, wrapped her arms around his neck, and hugged him to her. His palms ran up her back and he clutched her tightly.

Emotions from the past rose up in her, shifting from dark to light. She didn't know if the change was caused by discovering that Alex had shared the same heartfelt feelings for her back then as she had for him, or learning that losing him hadn't been her fault as she'd thought. But it made no matter. The knotted sentiments loosened and untangled and finally shook free. The memory of that fated summer was no longer something to be avoided; it became something to embrace.

After a long moment, he pulled back and stared into her face.

"I want to kiss you so bad right now," he whispered.

She felt his warm breath on her cheek, and she wanted nothing more than to feel his lips on hers.

"But there seems to be too many memories mucking up the air right now."

Josie grinned. "It'll pass. Memories have a way of ebbing and flowing like the tide."

They stood there, inches apart, just looking at each other.

Finally, he rubbed his hands together briskly. "It's cold out here. We should get in the car and turn the heater on. Are you hungry?"

"I'm starving."

"Let's go feast on fresh pasta."

Arm in arm, they made their way back to his car.

Chapter Eight

The small piles of bills stacked on the desk had been neatly sorted into $1s, $5s, $10s, and $20s. Josie had counted each stack three times, and now she was jotting down the sum total on the deposit slip. Before she made a bank run, she intended to take the deposit upstairs so Grams could look it over for herself. Having started out her banking career as a teller, Josie had become quite familiar with business deposits, and she was comfortable that she'd readied the transaction properly, but Joe's Place belonged to Grams and Josie felt it was the right thing to do to let her grandmother see the profits.

She was stuffing the money into the green bank bag when two sharp raps on the office door had her looking up. Alex smiled as he poked his head around the door.

"Customer?" she asked, automatically standing.

"No. Actually, the place is empty."

The bag *thunked* against the bottom of the desk drawer, and then Josie locked the drawer and pocketed the key.

"I'm sure it won't last long, but I think it's a good time for you to take a break," Alex told her, reaching out his hand to her. "It's a balmy 55 degrees outside and the sun is shining. Rare weather for this time of year. Want to slip outside with me and get some fresh air?"

"Did you say the sun is shining?" Josie laughed as she rounded the desk and slid her fingers into his. "You won't have to ask me twice."

Thirty seconds later, they were seated on the rough wooden bench that had sat there by the inlet for as long as Josie could remember.

"I'm pretty sure my granddaddy made this bench," Josie told him. "I've heard Grams say a hundred times that Granddad wanted to transform this area back here. He wanted to build a big patio with tables for outside eating. I think it would be great, sitting out here, eating lunch or dinner, watching the boat traffic going in and out of the bay."

"I never had the privilege of meeting Joe," Alex said.

She closed her eyes and lifted her face to the warmth of the sun. Chunks of ice clung to the riprap along the water's edge, groaning and heaving against the tide swell, proof that February had its claws hooked deep into Ocean City no matter how mild the air temperature might be.

"My memory of him is vague," she told Alex. "But I do know that he was the glue that held my mother and grandmother together. Mom and I didn't stay in town for very long after he died." She smoothed her palms up and down the thighs of her trousers.

"Is that when you moved to Rockville?"

Josie nodded. "Mom found a job in Housekeeping in a large hotel. She still works there as manager of the cleaning staff. I was sad to have to move away from the beach. I loved it so much. But I sure didn't miss all the squabbling between Grams and Mom."

The sound of footfalls on the wooden stairs leading to her grandmother's apartment drew

Josie's attention. The sight of Grams had her popping to her feet.

"Hey," she called out, "be careful up there. Where are you going?"

"Geneva called." Grams held the handrail and made her way slowly, one step at a time. "She and Judith asked me to come down to lunch. I'm feeling strong enough today, so I thought I'd join them."

"When are they coming?" Josie asked.

"Any minute, I think. They might be here already." Grams headed towards the back entrance of the restaurant.

Josie turned to Alex and murmured, "I hope she's not overdoing it. I'm going inside before Grams gets it into her head to carry a tray of drinks or something." The look in his eyes made her pause. "What?"

He smiled and shook his head. "I find your protective instincts rather sexy."

The compliment made her feel tingly inside. "Do you, now?"

Alex reached out and gave the hem of her coat a light tug. "You do know she's tough as nails, right?"

She offered him a silent nod, realizing the

question was his way of trying to assuage her worry over her grandmother's health.

Grams was just sliding into the booth next to one of her friends when Josie hurried across the dining room with glasses of water on a serving tray.

"Welcome to Joe's," Josie greeted.

"Josie, this is Judith Eversby," Grams said. "And Geneva Hartford."

"Ladies." Josie smiled.

"Surely, you remember us," Judith said. "We've been coming here to eat since you where just knee-high to a heron."

Geneva grinned. "Yes, you should remember us, seeing as how we haven't changed a lick over all these years."

"But you sure have changed," Judith crowed. "Deloris, your little Jojo has grown into a beautiful woman."

"Stop now," Josie said. "You're going make me blush."

"Beautiful and humble." Geneva looked across the table at Deloris. "You have good reason to be proud."

"I am," Grams said. "I had a little mishap and Josie came running. She's a wonderful granddaughter."

With a light touch on her grandmother's shoulder, Josie silently conveyed her deep affection. Then she looked at Geneva.

"You have a daughter named Sara, right?" Josie asked. "She used to baby sit me when I was a kid."

Geneva set her purse on the bench seat next to her. "Sara got married recently. She runs Sara's Sweet Shop on the boardwalk."

"I remember she had a couple of really good friends she used to hang out with." Josie tapped her chin with her index finger. "Cathy was the wild and crazy one. And the other was..."

"Heather," Geneva provided. "Cathy and Heather are still Sara's closest friends. In fact, Cathy owns the restaurant next to Sara's shop. It's called The Sunshine Grill. And Heather owns the B&B above, The Lonely Loon. All three of them are doing well."

"That's so good to hear," Josie said. "I'll have to stop in for a visit with them. They took me all up and down the boardwalk when I was a kid." Josie flipped open her small, ring-bound pad. "Now, how about if I take your orders and I can leave the three of you alone to talk?"

"Oh, yes," Judith said. "We have some talking to do."

"Um-hm." Geneva nodded. "We plan to give our friend Deloris a good scolding."

"Oh, Lord, save me," Grams muttered.

Thirty seconds later, Josie waltzed into the kitchen, tearing off the order and placing it on the metal turnstile that hung above the center island. The one slip of paper looked a little lonely up there all by itself, but keeping the routine, whether there was one order or eight, helped Alex stay organized and on task.

"One bowl of minestrone, one bowl of turkey noodle, and a Cobb salad," she told him. "I'll ladle out the soups, if you like, while you make the salad."

"Sounds like a plan."

Josie filled a bowl from one of the pots and then turned around just in time to see Alex's gaze shift upwards to hers. She stifled an inhalation. He'd been staring at her bottom. She was certain of it.

Her hip bumped the center island and half the contents of the bowl sloshed onto her. Chunks of tender turkey, wide egg noodles, and rounds of bright orange carrot rolled down the front of her, falling neatly into the deep pocket running along the bottom of her apron. She gasped and set the bowl on the island.

In a flash, Alex was in front of her. He reached around behind her and untied her apron strings. He deftly removed it and set the whole mess into the sink before the broth even had time to seep through the fabric.

"Good catch," he teased, returning to her with a towel, but finding her blouse dry and clean. "You couldn't do that again if you tried."

He was mere inches from her.

"You're probably right." Her tone was barely a whisper. "Alex, you shouldn't look at me like that when I'm trying to work."

The skin at the corner of his eyes crinkled when he grinned, and she didn't think she'd ever seen a man more handsome or more desirable.

"Are you calling me a safety hazard?"

Something in his tone sent delicious vibrations skittering along her spine and up into her scalp. She wanted to say *yes* because, when he was this close, she felt vulnerable. In a very good way.

"More l-like, um," she stammered, "a distraction."

Rather than back away from her, he held his ground. It was all she could do not to reach up and cup her hand against his cheek.

"Distractions are dangerous," she told him, "in a room filled with hot surfaces and sharp utensils."

His green eyes glittered with mischief. "You're right, of course. But, you know, we're going to have to deal with this at some point."

"Deal with what?"

"This... kiss we're both anticipating." He reached up and moved a tendril of her hair out of her eyes. "I can't speak for you, but if I don't get to taste your lips soon, I have no idea what might happen."

Happiness bloomed inside her chest like a summer rose.

She took a step away from him, grabbed a fresh bowl, and dipped into the pot. "You can speak for me," she quipped frankly. "But right now we have customers to feed."

"I'm on it."

Alex went back to his station and resumed assembling the salad, but his gaze continued to smolder. Josie felt the heat of it even though she was yards away.

Once he'd finished, he set the salad on Josie's tray next to the two bowls of soup, but he stopped her from picking it up. His palm was hot as his fingers curled around her upper arm.

"How about tonight?" he murmured.

"Isn't Emma's school dance tonight?"

He nodded. "I have to drop her off at the school at eight. Pick her up at ten."

Two hours, Josie thought. *Two glorious hours alone with him.*

"Can I drive up to your house a little early?" she asked. "I'd love to see Emma in her dress."

"Take the food out." He lifted the tray and handed it to her. "Then we'll make plans."

Josie fairly floated out to deliver lunch to her grandmother and her friends.

"I'm telling you, Deloris," Geneva said. "It's time for you to hand over the reins."

Grams splayed her hand on the tabletop. "I'm not ready to give it up completely. But I don't mind admitting that this heart thing is darned scary."

Feeling she was eavesdropping on a private conversation, Josie called out, "Here we go, ladies. Lunch is served."

As Josie placed the food on the table she was distinctly aware that the luscious warmth she'd felt just moments before was slowly chilled by the apprehension suddenly coiling in her belly. She'd been in Ocean City for nearly three weeks. Grams had been adamant that she would be fine, that she wanted to return to work in the diner just as soon as she was cleared by the doctor, that Joe's Place was her business—*her life*—and she was determined to run it. But now Josie knew that all of her grandmother's bluster and determination had been a sham.

Deloris Baxter was afraid.

Chapter Nine

"**D**ad, I know you have to bring in the snacks," Emma said from the back seat of the car, "but don't do anything to embarrass me."

Josie surreptitiously pressed her fingertips to her mouth to hide her smile and glanced over at Alex who had just turned into the parking lot of Emma's school. He glanced at his daughter in the rearview mirror.

"I promise not to pick my nose, Emma."

"Dad!"

The child was nervous, that was clear. "You're going to have a good time, Emma," Josie assured her. "Your dress is so cute. And your hair looks really good too."

"You really think so?" Emma asked.

"I do."

"There are no boys at this dance, right?" Alex teased.

Emma just rolled her eyes.

He pulled into a parking space and turned off the engine. His daughter bolted from the car as if it were on fire.

"Let me walk in alone, okay?" she said. "And don't come in when you come to pick me up. Just wait at the curb like all the other parents. I'll come out at ten."

She hurried toward the gymnasium doors as if she were in an Olympic walking race, and Alex watched her in silence. Finally, he looked at Josie over the roof of the sedan.

"I wonder if all the dads have cooties," he said. "Or is it just me?"

Offering him an empathetic tilt of her head, she told him. "With kids this age, I'd lay odds that *all* the parents have cooties."

"She's strung tighter than a banjo string."

Josie smiled. "She'll be fine just as soon as she hooks up with some of her friends."

He headed toward the back of the car. "Want to help me get the snacks inside?" he asked. "Then let's get back home. I have some candles to light and a glass of wine with your name in it."

"Josie Baxter," she said, standing soldier-straight near the trunk, "reporting for duty."

They were inside the school for less than ten minutes. Music blared and lights flashed. Big red hearts cut from poster board adorned with tissue paper, lace, and glitter decorated the wall behind the snack table. Helium balloons tied to weights sat in the center of the tables, swaying on their tethers. Alex looked around the gym for Emma, but she was lost in the throng of kids, laughing, talking, dancing, and milling about.

On their way back to the car, Alex glanced at Josie, his smile filled with promise and desire, and he held out his hand to her. Their fingers entwined as they headed across the parking lot, and excitement hummed through Josie like a low, sensual tune. He held onto her hand as they rounded to the passenger side of the car, but rather than open the door as she'd expected him to do, he forced her into a quarter-turn twirl.

"Ooo." The soft interjection was more an exhalation than a verbal cry. The door supported her back, and Josie found herself looking up into

Alex's face. She dipped her chin, gazed up at him through lowered lashes. "I wasn't expecting that."

"Good," he murmured. "I like to keep you on your toes."

He tucked his curled fingers beneath her jaw and guided her gaze fully onto his.

"I want you to tell me what's on your mind," he said. "You've been a little... I don't know... pensive all afternoon."

She blinked, surprised that he'd noticed. "It's Grams," she admitted. "I overheard her talking to her friends this afternoon. She said she's scared, Alex."

He didn't respond, just waited for more information.

"I think she's worried about more than just her health," Josie said. "I think she's worried about the diner. About the future. About..." Little jolts of anxiety squeezed a sigh from deep inside her.

"Well," he began, "I know Deloris would rather place her bare hand on a hot grill than admit to either one of us that she's frightened of anything. But considering that this was her second episode, I think it's only natural for her to be worried. Hell, Josie, we should all be worried."

She nodded. "I know. I do know that."

Absently, he toyed with a tendril of her hair, curling it around his index finger.

"What do you think she'd say if I were to offer to move back to Ocean City?"

It was an idea that had been rolling around in her mind all afternoon.

"You mean a permanent move?" he asked her. "You'd live here?"

"Yeah. I think it might be just what Grams needs. *If* she'll admit it."

"But what about your job in Rockville?"

Josie paused long enough to moisten her lips. "I've been thinking about that. You know, it's just a job. I mean, I'm very proud that I've risen in the ranks at the bank. But a career in banking was never my dream." Then she added, "To tell you the truth, I never really had a dream job."

She reached up and smoothed her fingers over the soft wool of his fine knit scarf. "But if I had the chance to come here, to be involved in a business that was started and built up by my family, well, I think that would be amazing."

He studied her face for a long moment. Then he said, "Having you here would be absolutely amazing."

Alex leaned forward, and the weight of his torso

felt so good to her. He smelled woodsy and clean, and Josie thought to herself that she'd go stark raving mad if he didn't kiss her.

Evidently, they were on the same wavelength because he whispered, "I have candles and wine and an oh-so-romantic Valentine's Day card waiting on you at my house, but I can't wait. I just can't."

His silky voice made her knees go soft and she was so relieved that the car door supported her from behind.

"Then don't wait another second," she breathed, lifting her mouth closer to his. "Please, don't."

When his lips touched hers, they were soft and hot and lusciously moist. Josie let her eyelids slide closed as her blood whooshed through her ears. His kiss was raw and needy, and she clutched at his scarf in an attempt to pull him closer. Josie parted her lips for him and he deepened the kiss.

Her head swam with saturating desire, and when he pulled away from her, she felt true disappointment.

He kissed her cheek and the tip of her nose. "You are so beautiful."

She smiled, and then she sucked in a slow, much-needed breath. As soon as she could think clearly again, she said, "Did I hear you say you bought me *another* Valentine's Day card?"

Relief glittered in his eyes. "I'm so glad you remembered."

"Are you kidding me?" she said. "That was the most romantic thing a sixteen-year-old could ever experience. *Ever.*"

"I went into that shop in the middle of the summer and asked for a Valentine's Day card and the owner looked at me like I was from Mars."

Josie felt the resonance of his chuckle through his leather coat.

"He really didn't want to be bothered with the love-sick kid that I was back then," he continued, "but I refused to be put off. I pestered that poor guy until he agreed to dig around in his stock for the perfect card."

The cold air condensed his breath as he talked, but Josie felt toasty warm.

"I can still remember what you wrote inside the card," she told him. "'*We won't be together on the most romantic day of the year, so let's make this the most romantic day.*'" As she recited the words that had emblazoned themselves on her memory all those summers ago, emotion compressed her heart.

"Alex, I fell for you so hard that night, it's a wonder I didn't break a couple of bones."

They chuckled, and then he kissed her again, long and lingering.

"I can't believe this." He trailed his fingers along the outer edge of her ear. "You have me feeling like a teenager again. It's like no time has passed at all. You've got my heart pounding like the hooves of a race horse."

She grinned and teased, "Oh, that's just because you haven't been with a woman in a while."

"No, sweetheart." He cupped her face between his hands. "This is because of you. Just you. All you."

The longing shining in his green eyes made Josie quiver. Moonlight glistened on his bottom lip, making her wish he'd kiss her again.

"Do you think," he said, "maybe we're being given a second chance?"

The question didn't need an answer, Josie decided, so she just let the hope and joy she felt churning inside her shine from her eyes and from her smile.

"Let's go back to my place," he suggested.

"Yes, please. I want to read my card." Feeling

emboldened, she added, "And then I want you to kiss me some more."

They were inside the car and Alex had started the engine when his cell phone rang. He pulled it from his coat pocket, looked at the screen, and frowned.

"It's Emma."

* * *

The ceiling fixtures inside the atrium beamed down a harsh, yellow light. Muffled music from inside the gymnasium thudded in the air. Mrs. Rue, the school principal stood to one side of the large double doors, standing close to Emma. Not three feet away from them stood a boy who was wearing his guilt as if it were a stiff Sunday suit.

Josie followed on Alex's heels in a bee line toward the threesome.

"What's going on?" Alex asked, his gaze going from his daughter to the principal and then back again.

"Mr. Thompson," the principal said, "I'm sorry about this, but Emma and Ryan have lost their privilege to attend tonight's dance. I'm sending them home."

Alex lifted one hand, palm up. "Emma, what

happened? What did you do? I didn't even have time to leave the parking lot."

"I didn't do anything, Dad," Emma exclaimed.

"You broke the rules, Emma," Principal Rue corrected firmly. Then she focused her attention on Alex. "She and Ryan left the building. I have security making the rounds outside, and the kids were found out on the bleachers by the track. I have to say, I'm very surprised, Mr. Thompson. I never would have expected this behavior from these two."

"There was no *behavior*," Emma said.

Alex's jaw tensed. "Stop being disrespectful, young lady. There are rules for a reason. Mrs. Rue is only trying to keep you safe. You know better." Then his attention swung to the boy. "And you—" Alex pointed at the kid "—I'll be calling your parents. You can be sure of that."

Josie ached for Emma as the child looked as if she wanted to shrivel up and disappear.

"Emma, apologize to Mrs. Rue," Alex said, sternness honing sharp edges on the order.

"I'm sorry."

"Consider yourself grounded," he told her. "For the next month, you're going nowhere, seeing no one. And give me your phone. No phone privileges either."

"But, Dad—"

Emma fell silent after one harsh look from Alex.

"Mrs. Rue," he said, "I'm very sorry. I want to assure you that Emma and I will be discussing this."

The principal nodded.

"Emma, get your coat and get in the car."

Alex turned and stormed toward the door, walking right past Josie as if she hadn't been standing there.

Chapter Ten

Instead of snuggling on the sofa with Alex as she'd imagined herself doing, Josie found herself sitting at his dining room table, cradling a mug of herb tea between her hands. She'd made one for herself and for Alex in the hopes of calming him down, but in the past fifteen minutes since they'd arrived at his house, he hadn't touched his.

"I just can't talk to her yet," he said, making his way to the window and looking out into the darkness.

But Josie suspected he was too peeved to actually notice anything that might be going on outside. The moment they'd entered the front door, Alex had sent Emma to her room and he'd been pacing and quietly fuming ever since.

"I mean, I'm not an idiot. I realized that raising a teenaged girl wasn't going to be easy." He turned to face Josie. "I figured Emma would go through a rebellious stage. That we'd have arguments. There would be butting of heads. That there would be times when I'd have to dole out some sort of punishment. That I'd have to come up with some strict discipline. That, as she matured, I'd have to be willing to change and negotiate the rules I set down." His eyes grew large. "But she's not even a teenager yet. I feel like my life as a parent has been completely turned upside down. And she's only twelve."

He stood in front of Josie now, the oak dining table between them, his hands gripping the back of the chair in front of him.

"Last week, she was manipulating me, through you, to do her bidding," he said. "And this week, she completely disregarded the rules and got herself kicked out of a school dance. What's next week going to bring?"

Realizing a rhetorical question when she heard one, Josie simply sat there offering him every ounce of empathy she could muster.

Alex gazed off through the doorway that led to the kitchen. "I don't know if I'm going to be able to do this. I'll never be able to watch her every second, or keep her from every bad thing that's out there, or—"

"Stop." The tiny word rushed from her mouth before Josie could prevent it. "Alex, I don't have any kids. I realize that. But I can't imagine there's a parent out there, single or not, who hasn't felt inadequate at some point. I can only imagine it comes with the territory." She slid the mug several inches away from her. "You love Emma very much. She knows that. Yes, she tried to manipulate you into taking me on a date, that's true. And she did get herself into trouble at school tonight. But those two things don't necessarily mean Emma is heading down some riotous road of rebellion. Like you said, she's only twelve. Maybe tonight was just a… simple mistake."

Josie noticed that he wasn't looking at her, and when she followed his gaze, she saw that he was focused on the lavender envelope that sat, unopened, in the center of the table. The Valentine's Day card he'd bought for her that represented a healing of the past and a promise of the future.

Alex bent at the waist and picked it up, and

when he straightened, resolve set his shoulders into a rigid line.

"When you came to me," he said, "and told me Emma was trying to contrive a date between us, I wanted to confront her. I wanted to tell her in no uncertain terms that my personal life was not her business to mess with. But instead of listening to my gut, I let you talk me into something else altogether." He tapped the envelope against the palm of his hand. "And now it sounds like you want me to believe that I'm making too much of her breaking the rules tonight."

The implication of what he was saying was like a sharp smack against her cheek. Josie's lips parted and she frowned.

"Alex, are you blaming me for what's happening with—"

"No," he said firmly. "I'm not blaming you. I'm blaming me. I allowed my focus to become... deflected."

The card slapped against the table when he dropped it.

"I think, for the foreseeable future, I need to narrow down my focus." He lifted his palms, holding them in a V shape. "I need to be the best father I can be for Emma. I need to work hard at the diner and earn enough money to get back to the place I was before cancer took Carin away from us. I need to take a step back. I need to figure out why my daughter is acting out. Whether it's that she's missing her mom or if it's just normal pre-adolescent defiance, that's for me to unravel and solve." He looked directly into Josie's eyes. "But right now, I have to remember what my priorities are and give them my undivided attention."

It was absolutely clear to Josie that those priorities did not include her. She slid back her chair and stood up.

"I understand," she said, relieved that the tremor coursing through her body didn't manifest itself in her voice. "I think it would be a good thing if I just grab my coat and go home."

"Dad?"

Alex turned to look at his daughter who was standing at the base of the stairs.

"I know you're mad at me," Emma said, her hands held into fists at her sides, her thumbs rubbing nervous circles against her index fingers. "I know I'm in trouble. And I'm supposed to stay in my room. But I think you're about to do something really, really wrong."

Alex didn't respond.

"You shouldn't be mad at Josie," Emma said.

Standing behind Alex, Josie watched his spine straighten. "Listen here, young lady, you will not tell me what to think or how to act. I'm the parent. You are the child."

Emotion welled up in Emma's eyes, spilling huge teardrops onto her cheeks. "Daddy, I know you said we'd talk tomorrow, but I was telling the truth at the school when I said I didn't mean to break the rules. Ryan likes Chloe and he asked me to ask her if she would be his girlfriend." Emma clasped her hands in front of her. "But Chloe doesn't like Ryan, Dad. She likes Jonas. I just wanted to find a quiet place to explain everything to Ryan. I knew he was going to feel bad. We didn't even think about the rules when we went outside."

Alex's shoulders relaxed. "Honey, I'm proud of you for caring about Ryan's feelings. But that doesn't change the fact that you broke the rules. The rules are there for a reason."

"I know, Dad," Emma said. "And I'm really sorry."

Emma's green gaze met Josie's, and in the hopes of offering the child some support, Josie smiled. But surprisingly, Emma only became more upset.

Her chin trembled and fresh tears rolled down her face.

"I don't know what contrive means," Emma said to her dad, "but I only asked Josie about going out on a date with you because I wanted you to find a friend."

Alex turned and looked at Josie, slight panic shadowing his gaze. He turned back to his daughter. "Emma, just how long have you been listening to my conversation with Josie?"

The child heaved a sigh and then admitted. "I wanted a drink of water, but when I was on the steps, I heard that sound in your voice. Like you were trying to bend a steel pole with just your words. I-I haven't heard that for a while. Ever since Josie came to work in the diner, you've been... different. Happier. But tonight I heard it again when you were talking to her. And... and I don't like it."

Emma's brow puckered as she tried to put her thoughts into words. "Ever since Mom got sick, you've been really sad. After she left us, you encouraged me to go out with my friends, shopping or to the movies or just hang out or whatever. And I knew you were trying to make me feel better. But you never did any of those things for yourself. You just kept feeling sad. Mommy loved us, Dad. She didn't want to leave us. But she wouldn't want you to feel so sad. You worry about money, and the diner, and Miss Deloris, and me. You worry too much."

A sob wrenched from her throat and she ran to her father, burying her face against his diaphragm and wrapping her arms around his waist.

Her voice was muffled as she said, "Please let Josie be your friend, Daddy. Please."

Alex scooped his distraught daughter into his arms and then turned to look at Josie. "I'm going to take her upstairs."

Josie nodded. "I'll bring a glass of water and a cool washcloth." His gaze never left hers, so she assured him, "And then I'll go."

A small frown nipped at the space between his eyebrows. "Please stay. I'd like to talk to you."

* * *

Josie sat alone in Alex's living room for nearly half an hour waiting for him. Poor little Emma had been crying into her pillow, her father sitting on the edge of the mattress comforting her as he could, when Josie had taken the water and a damp washcloth upstairs. Appreciation had glowed in Alex's eyes.

"I'll be down soon," he'd promised.

Raising a child was a labyrinthine endeavor, Josie decided, filled with complex issues and problems that a parent could never fully anticipate or prepare for. The mere notion of the job Alex faced as Emma's father seemed overwhelming. But one thing was certain; he loved that child with every fiber of his being. And he would protect her to the best of his ability.

Soft footfalls on the steps drew Josie's gaze and she watched as Alex came into view. His smile was temperate and unreadable as he came over and sat down on the sofa next to her.

"It's been months since she's cried herself to sleep," he said.

"I'm sorry." The apology was the first thing that popped into Josie's head.

"Don't be. None of this is your fault."

He reached over and covered her hand with his. Josie couldn't help but feel surprised and she knew her face showed it.

"I know, I know," Alex groaned. "I was the one who got it wrong. Can you ever forgive me?"

She didn't answer him, just looked into his face.

Alex shook his head and glanced up toward the

ceiling. "Do you know how humbling it is to be bested by a twelve year old?"

His attempt at lightening the mood fell flat. The tension inside Josie was still too intense.

"Everything Emma said was true. Everything. You've changed me, Josie. Emma was right. In the three short weeks since you came to Ocean City, I've been a happier man. I can't deny it." His voice softened as he added, "I don't want to deny it."

He lifted her hand to his lips and pressed a soft kiss on her knuckles.

The muscles in her back and shoulders began to relax and she was able to take a full breath for the first time in many minutes.

"Can you ever forgive me?" he asked. "I lost my head earlier tonight. My parental incompetence got the better of me. I can't explain it. I guess I was looking for a scapegoat and you were right there in front of me." He looked wretched. "Nothing that's happened is your fault, Josie. I know you have only tried to help me. I'm very sorry."

"It's okay," she told him. "Really."

His face pinched. "Have I ruined everything? Between us, I mean?"

She smiled and answered him with a shake of her head.

"Wait right here."

He let go of her hand, stood up, and headed into the dining room. When he returned, he had the lavender envelope in his hand.

Alex sat down, closer to her this time, and set the card on her lap.

"I can't believe I nearly messed up my second chance," he told her.

Josie slid her palm over the smooth surface of the envelope. "We have Emma to thank for the save, I guess."

"We do," he agreed. He shifted next to her. "Before Emma fell asleep, she made me promise to ask you a question."

Josie arched her brows.

"Will you be my friend?"

Joy seeped through her, bright and warm as sunshine. "I'd love to be your friend."

His kiss started off sweet and sensuous, but quickly grew deliciously ravenous, and Josie knew they would be so much more than friends.

Epilogue

Josie pulled into a parking spot behind the diner and turned off her car engine. Tulips and crocuses left punches of color in the bright planters that lined the brand new outside eating area that was nearly complete. Spring sunshine warmed the salt-tinged air and soon diners would be enjoying their meals outside as they watched the fishermen, sailboats, and pontoons come and go through the inlet. The deck would offer extra seating which, in turn, would mean more income for the diner, and Josie marveled at how the business had changed in just a couple of months. She'd barely gotten the car door open when Emma came barreling out of the back door, racing across the fine wood planking toward her.

"Welcome home!" Emma shouted. "Look what I made for you while you were gone."

The bracelet had been constructed of interwoven threads in various shades of blue with delicate glass beads arranged in an intricate pattern. Josie let Emma slip it onto her wrist next to the three others she already wore.

"It's beautiful, Emma," Josie said. "Prettier than I could ever find in a jewelry store."

"You think so?"

"I really do." Josie turned her hand, this way and that, admiring her new present.

Emma beamed.

"Have you been taking good care of Smokey?" Josie asked.

"Yes," Emma said. "I've fed him every day and kept his water dish full. And I've learned how much cats love to chase a flashlight beam. Don't tell Chloe, but Smokey's my best friend." Then she wrinkled her nose. "Cleaning his litter box isn't my favorite job."

Josie laughed. "Mine, either. Want to help me carry some stuff inside?"

"So this is it?" Emma asked. "You don't have to go away again?"

"This is it. When I unpack this stuff, I'll be a permanent resident of Ocean City.

The three days she'd spent in Rockville had been the fifth and final trip she'd taken over the past few weeks to clean out her apartment and finalize her move.

"I'll help you," Emma said. "But Dad and Miss Deloris want you to come inside the diner first."

The mere thought of seeing Alex sent elation spiraling through her like a prima ballerina on tiptoe. She stepped away from the car and shut the door. "How could they think I wouldn't come inside to say hello?" A teasing tone ruffled through the question.

When she started toward the back door, Emma blocked her way.

"They want you to come around the front." The child's voice dropped to an excited whisper. "They have a surprise for you."

Josie's face lit up. "I think we should hurry then."

The two of them took the sidewalk around to the front of the building, and the instant they rounded the corner, Josie noticed something different about the building. She gave the huge picture window a double take. Her grandmother stood inside, wearing a big grin. But then Josie noticed the words on the window. The red decals that read *Joe's Place* just three days ago had been replaced by large, bright, lemon yellow letters that spelled out *Jojo's Place*.

Josie froze to the spot, sudden tears blurring her vision. She mouthed silently to Grams through the glass, "*What did you do?*"

Grams disappeared from the window only to show up again as she pushed her way outside through the front door. "Josie, please don't be upset." The elderly woman swiped her own misty eyes with a tissue. "The diner is going to be yours eventually. You might as well start working on name recognition now." Grams turned to look up at the window, pride straightening her torso. "Your granddaddy would approve, I'm sure."

The hug the two women shared expressed the deep love they felt for each other. Ever since Josie had approached her grandmother back in the winter about moving to Ocean City, their relationship had become closer than ever. Josie's desire to learn the ropes of the restaurant business had given Deloris Baxter a whole new lease on life.

Alex came outside to join them on the sidewalk.

"Hey," he greeted her softly. "Are you surprised?"

"Surprised?" Josie said. "More like totally overwhelmed." She couldn't keep the happy tears from spilling down her cheeks.

"Dad, Josie likes her bracelet," Emma said.

"I don't just like it," Josie said. "I love it."

Alex wrapped his arms around her, and Josie held tight as he pulled her snugly up against him.

"How long have you known about this?" she whispered in his ear.

His eyes twinkled with mischief when he leaned back and looked into her face. "Since before Deloris had her procedure. She made me promise that, if something happened to her, you were to get the diner."

"Nothing's going to happen to me," Grams grumbled. "I'm so fit I could tap dance from here all the way to the boardwalk. But I don't have time for such foolishness. I've got customers to serve. Emma, come inside and help me."

Once they were alone outside, Alex tipped up Josie's chin. "I'm so glad you're home. I've missed you like you wouldn't believe."

"I've missed you, too."

Their kiss was sweet and filled with unspoken promises. As winter had given way to spring, they had spent every free moment together. Their affection for one another swelled like an ever rising tide that grew stronger with each passing day.

"I love you," he said.

Josie smiled, closed her eyes, and pressed her forehead to his, fearful that the happiness rising inside her would choke off her ability to speak. She would never tire of hearing him say those three little words even if she lived to be a hundred and five years old.

"I love you, too," she was finally able to say.

She gazed into the sea green eyes of the man who owned her heart, and she knew that she was home.

A Note From The Author

Dear Reader,

When I was in my late teens, my boyfriend at the time (he's my husband now!) gave me a beautiful porcelain heart with a poem engraved inside an intricate knot. The words touched my heart. They said, "Accept this token that I send, a knot of love without an end. A cord embraced and intertwined as doth my love if you'll be mine. For you my pretty Valentine." Now, you must understand. My husband is a straight-arrow, scientist-type. He's not a romantic. But when he does something, he gets it right. (I'm smiling right now.) His gesture will always be, in my mind, the most romantic thing any man has ever done. I hope the love of your life touches your heart this Valentine's Day.

With Love,

Donna Fasano

A Note From The Author

Let's keep in touch!

Find me on the web:

My Website

On Facebook

On Twitter

Sign up for my Newsletter

Joe's Place Chili

6 strips smoked bacon, diced

1 lb lean ground beef, cooked in separate skillet, drained

2 cups onions, diced

2 stalks celery, diced

1 green pepper, seeded and diced

1 jalapeño pepper, seeded and minced (optional)

2 14.5-ounce can fire-roasted tomatoes (with juice)

1 15-ounce can tomato puree

2 cloves garlic, minced

3 tablespoon chili powder

2 teaspoons cumin

1 teaspoon salt

1/2 teaspoon black pepper

1/2 teaspoon smoked paprika, (optional)

2 15-ounce cans kidney bean, rinsed and drained

1 cup water

Directions:

1. Cook bacon in a large pot until crisp. Remove from pot and set aside to be used as a topping.
2. Add browned beef, onions, celery, and peppers to the bacon grease and cook until onions are translucent, approximately 10-15 minutes, stirring occasionally.
3. Add fire-roasted tomatoes, puree, garlic, and spices, beans, and water. Bring to a simmer. Cook over low heat, stirring occasionally, for 1-2 hours.

Serve with your choice of toppings: crisp bacon, sour cream, shredded cheddar cheese, thinly sliced scallion.

Alex's Heart Healthy Chili

2 medium zucchinis, chopped

1 lb mushrooms, sliced

1 large onion, diced

2 stalks celery, diced

2 carrots, peeled and chopped

1 red pepper, seeded and chopped

1 yellow pepper, seeded and chopped

1/2 cup fresh parsley, minced fine

2 14.5-ounce can fire-roasted tomatoes (with juice)

1 15-ounce can tomato puree

3 cloves garlic, minced

3 tablespoon chili powder

2 teaspoons cumin

1 teaspoon cinnamon

1 teaspoon oregano

1 teaspoon salt

Alex's Heart Healthy Chili

1/2 teaspoon black pepper

1/2 teaspoon smoked paprika

1 15-ounce can cannellini beans (white kidney beans), rinsed and drained

1 15-ounce can black beans, rinsed and drained

1 cup vegetable juice (example V8 Juice) or water

Directions:

1. Add vegetables, fire-roasted tomatoes, and puree to a large pot and stir to combine.
2. Add remaining ingredients. Bring to a simmer. Cook over low heat for 1-2 hours.
3. Serve with toppers: sour cream, shredded cheddar cheese, sliced scallions.

Alex's Jalapeño Cornbread

1 cup yellow corn meal

1 cup all-purpose flour

2 teaspoons baking powder

1 teaspoon salt

1/2 teaspoon fresh cracked black pepper (optional)

1 cup milk

1 egg, beaten

1 teaspoon liquid smoke

1/4 cup olive oil

1-2 jalapeños (depending on desired spice level), seeded and minced

Directions:

1. Preheat oven to 400° F. Add corn meal, flour,

baking powder, salt, and pepper to a bowl. Stir to thoroughly combine.

2. In a separate bowl, whisk together milk, egg, liquid smoke, and oil.

3. Add wet ingredients to dry ingredients. Stir only until incorporated. Do not over mix.

4. Add jalapeños to batter and stir to evenly incorporate.

5. Pour batter into a greased 8-inch square pan and spread into an even layer. Bake for 25 minutes or until a wooden pick inserted into the center comes out clean.

Meatloaf – Joe's Place
Thursday Special

1/3 cup dry breadcrumbs

1/3 cup oatmeal

1 cup milk

2 lbs lean ground beef

2 eggs, slightly beaten

1 medium onion, minced

1 clove garlic, minced

2 tablespoons Worcestershire Sauce

1 teaspoon salt

1/2 teaspoon black pepper

Glaze

1/4 cup ketchup

3 tablespoon dark brown sugar

Meatloaf – Joe's Place Thursday Special

Directions:

1. Mix all meatloaf ingredients in a large bowl until well incorporated.
2. Place meatloaf mixture in a loaf pan that's been sprayed with cooking spray.
3. Bake in a pre-heated 350° F oven for 30 minutes.
4. While meatloaf is in the oven, mix together the glaze ingredients in a small bowl.
5. Remove meatloaf from oven, spread glaze over the top, and put back into the oven to bake for another 20 minutes or until the center is no longer pink (160° F on a meat thermometer).

Sour Cream Bashed Potatoes – Joe's Place Thursday Special

3 lbs red-skinned potatoes, washed and cut into 1-inch cubes (do not peel)

Salt

1 1/4 cups milk

6 tablespoons butter, room temperature

1/2 – 3/4 cup sour cream

1/2 teaspoon black pepper

1 scallion, thinly sliced (optional)

Directions:

1. Place potatoes in a large pot and cover with cold water. Add 2 tablespoons salt and bring to a boil. Turn down the heat to medium and simmer for about 10 to 12 minutes or until the potatoes are tender when poked with a fork.

Sour Cream Bashed Potatoes – Joe's Place
Thursday Special

2. While potatoes are cooking, place the milk and butter in a saucepan over medium heat until the butter is melted, stirring occasionally. Turn off heat and set aside.

3. When the potatoes are tender, drain them well and return potatoes to the pot. Add the warm milk/butter mixture, 1/2 cup of the sour cream, 1 to 2 teaspoons salt (to taste), and the black pepper. Use a hand-held potato masher to "bash" the potatoes. If potatoes seem too dry, and the extra 1/4 cup of sour cream and stir to combine. This dish should be lumpy and rustic, not smooth and creamy. Top with thinly sliced scallion, if desired.

Breakfast Casserole

1 lb mild pork sausage

1 lb hot pork sausage

1 30-ounce package frozen hash brown potatoes

1 1/2 teaspoons salt

1/2 teaspoon black pepper

1 1/2 cups sharp cheddar cheese, grated

6 large eggs

1 3/4 cups milk

Directions:

1. Fry sausage in a skillet, breaking up into crumbles, until no longer pink. Remove from skillet and drain thoroughly.
2. In the same skillet, prepare hash browns according to package directions, using 1/2

teaspoon of the salt and 1/4 teaspoon of the black pepper.

3. In a large bowl, stir together the hash browns, the sausage, and the cheese until thoroughly combined. Pour into a lightly greased 13-inch by 9-inch baking pan.

4. Whisk together the eggs, the milk, the remaining 1 teaspoon salt and 1/4 teaspoon black pepper. Pour egg mixture evenly over potato mixture.

5. Bake in a pre-heated 350° F oven for 35 to 40 minutes or until top is golden brown.

Deloris Baxter's French Toast

2 eggs

    1/2 cup milk

    1 tablespoon sugar

    1 teaspoon vanilla extract

    1/2 teaspoon cinnamon

    8 slices of hearty white bread

Directions:

1. In a shallow container, whisk together the eggs, milk, sugar, vanilla, and cinnamon until thoroughly combined and sugar is dissolved.
2. Dip bread slices in egg mixture, coating both sides evenly.
3. Fry bread slices in a heated skillet or on a griddle over medium heat until both sides are

golden brown and egg coating is cooked through.

4. Serve with butter and maple syrup.

Lemon Queen Pie

1 prepared 9-inch deep dish pie crust

Lemon Filling
1 1/4 cups sugar
6 tablespoons cornstarch
1/4 teaspoon salt
1 cup water
2 tablespoon butter
3 teaspoons grated lemon peel (yellow part only)
3/4 cup fresh lemon juice

Cream Cheese Filling
3 4-ounce packages cream cheese
3/4 cup confectioner's sugar
1 1/2 cups non-dairy whipped topping, thawed
1 tablespoons fresh lemon juice

Lemon Queen Pie

Directions:

1. Bake pie crust in a pre-heated 450° F oven for 10-14 minutes or until golden brown. Remove from oven and set aside to cool.
2. Prepare lemon filling: In a saucepan, whisk together the sugar, cornstarch, and salt. Add the water, butter, lemon peel, and lemon juice. Cook over medium heat, stirring constantly, until mixture comes to a rolling boil. Remove from heat and set aside to cool.
3. Prepare the cream cheese filling: Beat together the cream cheese and confectioner's sugar until smooth. Fold in the whipped topping and the lemon juice.
4. Assemble the pie: Spread the cream cheese filling evenly in the bottom of the pie crust. Top with the cooled lemon filling and spread evenly. Refrigerate for 4 hours or overnight.

Rich Chocolate Pecan Bars

Crust:

1 1/4 cups (2 1/2 sticks) unsalted butter, room temperature

6 tablespoons granulated sugar

2 large eggs

1 1/2 teaspoons vanilla extract

2 1/4 cups all-purpose flour

1/4 teaspoon baking powder

1/2 teaspoon salt

   Topping:

1/2 pound (2 sticks) unsalted butter

1/2 cup light corn syrup

1 1/2 cups light brown sugar, packed

1 1/2 cups semi-sweet chocolate pieces

1 pound pecans, chopped

Directions:

Rich Chocolate Pecan Bars

1. For the crust: Cream the butter and granulated sugar in the bowl until light and fluffy. Add eggs and vanilla and mix well. Add the flour, baking powder, and salt. Stir until well combined. Press the dough evenly into an ungreased 13 inch x 9 inch baking pan, making a small lip around the edge like you would a pie crust. Dough will be sticky; sprinkle the dough and your hands lightly with flour. Bake in a pre-heated 350° F oven for 15 minutes, until the crust is set but not browned.

2. While crust is baking, prepare the topping: Combine the butter, corn syrup, and brown sugar in a saucepan. Over medium heat, stir constantly until mixture comes to a boil. Simmer for 3 minutes. Remove from heat. Add the semi-sweet chocolate and pecans, stirring until chocolate melts. Pour topping over the crust and spread the filling evenly, staying within the lip of the crust. Bake at 350° F for 25 to 30 minutes, until the filling is set. Remove from the oven and allow to cool. Cut into bars and serve. Wrap remaining bars in an air-tight container and store in the refrigerator.

Other Books by Donna Fasano

Ocean City Boardwalk Series:
Following His Heart, Book 1
Two Hearts In Winter, Book 2
Wild Hearts of Summer, Book 3
An Almost Perfect Christmas, Book 4
Grown-Up Christmas List, Book 5
The Wedding Planner's Son, Book 6
Second Chance Valentine, Book 7

~ ~ ~

Reclaim My Heart
The Merry-Go-Round
Her Fake Romance
Take Me, I'm Yours
His Wife for a While
Mountain Laurel

~ ~ ~

The Single Daddy Club Series:

Other Books by Donna Fasano

Derrick, Book 1
Jason, Book 2
Reece, Book 3

~ ~ ~

A Family Forever Series:
A Beautiful Stranger, Book 1
Made in Paradise, Book 2
A Reason to Believe, Book 3
An Accidental Family, Book 4
Nanny and the Professor, Book 5

~ ~ ~

Non-fiction Books
Cooking In All Directions
Prayer of Quiet
Favorite Christmas Cookies
Recipes of Love
Guy Food

About the Author

Donna Fasano is a USA TODAY Bestselling Author whose books have sold 4 million copies worldwide and have been translated into two dozen languages. She lives on Maryland's Eastern Shore with her husband.

www.ingramcontent.com/pod-product-compliance
Lightning Source LLC
Chambersburg PA
CBHW030305130626
46549CB00002B/707